THE PARTY'S OVER

"My God," Brock whispered when he saw the girdle of bright red sticks cinched tightly around Paine's waist. There were wires linking them together along the top. The eye in the DCI's mind filled with hellish visions worthy of Hieronymous Bosch: bleeding body parts, screams of agony and hysteria, a reprise of Hiroshima beneath the bright blue Maryland summer sky.

"Before you beckon to any of Berghold's boys," Paine suggested evenly, "you might want to think about how loud you want this party to get."

"You really are insane!" Brock's eyes were riveted to the dynamite.

"Crazy enough," Paine said, slipping his hand casually inside his coat. "What'll it be, Brock? Shall we liven things up around here?"

ROGUE AGENT #4

LAST RITES

JACK DRAKE

AVON BOOKS ◆ NEW YORK

ROGUE AGENT #4: LAST RITES is an original publication of Avon
Books. This work has never before appeared in book form. This work is
a novel. Any similarity to actual persons or events is purely coincidental.

AVON BOOKS
A division of
The Hearst Corporation
1350 Avenue of the Americas
New York, New York 10019

First Avon Books Printing: August 1991

AVON TRADEMARK REG. U.S. PAT. OFF. AND IN OTHER COUNTRIES,
MARCA REGISTRADA, HECHO EN U.S.A.

Printed in the U.S.A.

RA 10 9 8 7 6 5 4 3 2 1

1

John Paine dropped from the fire escape onto the sidewalk as lightly as any 230-pound man could. Behind him the nasty crackle of gunfire continued in the vicinity of the hotel. It was hardly an unusual sound in that portion of Manhattan, the Lower East Side, but even in that savage setting, it was not likely to go unnoticed by the perpetual police presence for too long.

Knowing this, Paine did not linger. But once his feet hit the littered street, neither did he run. To run was to attract attention. Instead he strolled. Listening closely for even the slightest resonance of pursuit. Who had found him this time, and how? he wondered. There was no way for him to know. He could only hope whoever it was did not survive to carry on the chase. But if they did, he had a new identity in mind that should throw them off the scent. For a few days, at least. He needed time. Time to think. About the mole.

A traitor was hidden among the ranks of his employer, the Central Intelligence Agency. Someone who had managed somehow to set in motion a chain of events that had driven John Paine out into the cold, branded as a renegade. A once-trusted field operative who must now die for the mortal sin of disobedience.

As he stepped lightly over the still form of a Hispanic male who was either taking a break or dead, Paine wondered how many people were dedicated to his demise, how many more killers would come after him. A cruiser shrieked past him, headed for the cockroach farm he'd just fled, and Paine vowed that he would be ready for them, regardless of their number, regardless of how good they might be. He didn't consider himself the best, though there were some in the trade who viewed him that way.

He knew that humility was the most valuable survival skill he possessed, over the long haul. As in most other sectors of life, pride directly preceded a fall. And when killing was your business, the falls were usually the kind from which you didn't recover. So Paine was content to leave the pleasures of arrogance to the competition. To his way of thinking, "modest and breathing" was much preferable to "vain and not."

While Paine put distance between himself and the recent near-miss, the NYPD was busy learning how much trouble a pair of career cutthroats could be.

When Samson had slaughtered his way through Paine's recruited sentries in the alley behind the hotel, he had done it as quietly as only a truly gifted butcher could. He was a virtuoso with a spear at close quarters. The smirking delinquents who'd laughed at his diminutive size had been no more than sperms and eggs in strangers when the merc had begun the study of kendo.

Samson had nearly chosen a samurai sword to postpone the gunplay instead of the spear. In the end, however, he'd decided it was too obvious.

That was a shame. With it, he could have made the final moments of the punks ever so much more interesting than they had been. In the proper hands, such a weapon was transformed into a great Cuisinart, a whizzing slice-and-dice machine, which could disassemble an individual so swiftly that the victim would not live long enough to appreciate the process.

All of his stealth had been rendered pointless, however, when the shots reverberated in the street on the hotel's other side. Then Samson had known he was running out of time as he seized the silenced Uzi that lay concealed beneath his Goodwill overcoat. For a moment, he'd considered scrubbing the mission; calling it off as one of those times when a good plan was blown by unforseeable events.

But instinct had urged him to proceed. So he did. Only to be confronted moments later by a wiry, boyish bitch in hot pants who handled a Heckler & Koch P7 nine-millimeter automatic far better than any woman who made a living by turning big ones into little ones should. In the instant before she'd swung the muzzle toward him, Samson had failed to recognize the face, but the form was only too familiar. The practiced, predatory way she moved had "professional" inscribed into every gesture. Somehow the two of them had managed a masterpiece of bad timing, making their separate, independent attempts on Paine at precisely the same moment.

Samson found their accidental folly amusing, but the humorless "hooker" forced him to dive for cover before he could share the joke with her and put a few chunky slugs into her lithe physique.

As Samson assumed, Martina Vlota found his sudden appearance less than hilarious. Like him, a mere glimpse was enough to recognize another of her kind. Even as she fired at the gnome's darting shape, she cursed the gridlock of enemies the bastard Paine seemed to attract. She wanted the sadistic brute to herself. She had earned that much after the horror he had put her through. But the army of all the others who hungered for his bones seemed committed to forcing her to share the cold flavor of her revenge with them.

As she vented her frustration with each accurate shot at Samson, Vlota clung to the desperate hope that her quarry would choose to fight, not flee. But as the minutes passed since she'd wasted the horny goons guarding the front door, she was forced to acknowledge that the wily rogue had opted for discretion instead.

Though the understanding came as a disappointment, it was hardly a surprise. It was Paine's reflexive caution that had been Vlota's undoing at the start. There'd been no apparent reason for him to wear the Kevlar on that balmy night when she'd shot him in the midst of the Adriatic Sea. She had successfully camouflaged herself among the crew, passing herself off as a male steward as only an androgynous sexual chameleon could.

So Vlota had assumed he wasn't wearing it. When he collapsed onto the deck, she had been certain of her triumph, confident that she could hover over him to deliver the make-sure shot and savor it as her reward for a job well done. And it was then that Paine had erupted into life beneath her, lifting her with his brawny legs and kicking her like so much flailing garbage to eventual death by drowning in the rolling, salty wilderness below.

But Vlota had been too strong and a little too lucky to die, and she had a ravenous appetite for revenge that helped to keep her afloat.

Now another chance for repayment had been

ruined, and she knew the ever-mounting siren screams meant that her chances of escape were dwindling by the second. And Paine was slipping further away, his trail growing cold and losing its scent.

Samson's train of thought, as he returned her fire with repeated short, muffled bursts, was very much the same. He wanted her dead as badly as she craved the same for him, but first things first. It wouldn't do to let one's priorities get confused.

Therefore, when he saw Vlota backing toward the front entrance, he let her go, knowing she still stood a strong chance of being killed by the arriving police. On the other hand, so did he. As adept at and inclined toward murder as he might be, Samson knew he was not supernatural. He was a force of one. The NYPD, whatever skill they might lack, numbered in the thousands.

From the sound of the accumulating chorus of wails coming from every direction, it seemed as if half of them had decided to show up for the party.

Vlota had just emerged onto the hotel's front steps when the first blue-and-white made a wailing, skidding crash stop in the street. Without the purse, stashing the H & K was something of a challenge. Her body was spare, and the little she wore was hardly more than another layer of skin. She settled for stuffing the compact nine-millimeter between her stretchy waistband and her spine.

Then the Albanian assassin went into her act with a long, skull-piercing scream.

"He's killing everyone! Mary, Mother of God! There's blood everywhere!" She staggered down the steps toward them, taking pains to keep her back close to the wall. Vlota pressed a hand to each side of her head, as if trying to contain the boiling hysteria within.

One of the two patrolmen who'd emerged from the cruiser advanced on the hotel entrance, waving the hooker out of the way, crouching with his gun held high and ready. He was buying her performance. Maybe not completely. He'd been a cop in New York too long to assume that any prostitute was nonviolent. But enough to allow Vlota to crab sideways down the sidewalk, fearing that John Paine was surely long gone by then. As disturbing as she found the prospect of losing him, she knew she must concentrate for the moment on her escape. She must keep the victim act going until she was safely away. Then she would have to find him again. She thought she knew how she would do that; do it in a way that would hurt the man she loathed in more ways than one.

Vlota could hardly wait.

"Careful, Jimmy!" The partner who'd remained behind the opened door of the cruiser, covering the entrance with a sawed-off twelve-gauge pump, barked the warning as a score and more patrol cars arrived. Most took up positions in the street, but several crowded into the alley behind the building, as well.

As soon as the Albanian spotted a cruiser with a lone cop behind the wheel, she hurried over to it, hugging herself with both arms and whimpering convincingly. She had to force herself not to look behind her. That would seem suspicious, she thought. She would have to trust to the luck that appeared to have deserted her recently. If a cop got behind her and saw the menacing silhouette riding her tail ... she was finished.

But so was he. And as many of his pals as she could take with her before the end.

"Oh, Jesus, Officer! I'm so scared!" she said to

him. He was young and handsome. Vlota noted the way his eyes dropped for an instant to her long, hard legs.

"What's going on in there?" he asked.

"There's a nut with a machine gun. He's blowing everyone away. I don't know how I got out alive!" She loaded her voice and expression with all the vulnerable appeal she could muster.

"Why don't you get in the back. You'll be safer there." The officer reached over the seat to open the door for her.

"Sounds good to me," Vlota said. She hopped into the rear of the cruiser, pulling the door closed as soon as she had drawn her legs inside.

"It's a good thing you got out of there alive," the rookie said as he turned around on the seat to get a better look at her. "A good body is a terrible thing to waste."

"You like what you see?" she asked, reaching behind her back casually as his eyes visited various points of interest.

"You could say that, yeah," he replied.

When her hand reappeared grasping the stubby nine, the cop suddenly lost interest in everything but the bore.

"How about life? You like that, too?" Vlota inquired, keeping the automatic beneath the level of the window next to her, aiming at the point on the seat between the P7 and his heart.

It came too late, but the youth finally realized the woman was not what she seemed. "Sure do," he said evenly. "It's gotten to be a regular habit."

"Then get me out of here, and don't get cute while you're at it. We get stopped, you get shot ... several times. My word on it. Now turn around. Maybe if you're good, you'll live to make a pass at someone who's impressed," Vlota said.

He did as he was told. "Consider this a cab."

7

"Don't worry. I do," she responded.

Samson was in the alley behind the hotel when cruisers sealed it off at both ends. He was too much the warrior not to consider blasting his way through them, at least briefly. Then common sense prevailed. He really stood to lose very little by surrendering. He had already made sure of that.

So when they saw him there, and bellowed their commands, Samson reluctantly complied. He tossed the Uzi onto the grimy pavement where they could see it, and followed it with the Python he was carrying as backup. Then he dropped to his knees, laced his fingers behind his head, and waited as a dozen blue suits approached him from both directions.

The first cop to draw near almost shot Samson when he got a good look at his face. It was a hellish reconstructed landscape that provoked such violent reactions wherever it appeared.

"You twitch, and I'll make you uglier than you already are, pal," the cop said.

"Sticks and stones, Officer. Sticks and stones," Samson replied softly as the left side of his mouth twitched up to reveal his fine, white teeth.

"I think we need an exorcist," another cop said.

"You give ugly a whole new meaning, little dude." The third officer had picked up the Uzi and was aiming it at Samson's chest.

"Sort of what you do for stupid, right?" Samson replied with a dry chuckle.

"You have the right to remain silent—" one of them began, but Samson cut him off.

"Skip it. I'm a government agent," he said.

"Like hell you are," the one with the Uzi said with total disbelief.

"You could say that, but it's beside the point. I have a document to show you, and a number for

8

you to call. Then I will be on my way," Samson said.

And he assumed it would be that simple. But he was in New York City, where things did not always go according to plan.

So it was not.

2

The clerk finally returned from the stockroom into which he'd disappeared some minutes before. When he handed Paine the suit coat he'd found, a forty-eight long, his expression was triumphant.

"It's a rare occasion when I'm called on to fit an individual of your size. I really wasn't sure if I could handle it, but I think this will do the trick. How do the pants fit?" He held the coat so Paine could work his bulk into it.

"Fine," Paine replied as he studied his reflection in the full-length mirror in front of him.

"Is something wrong?" the clerk asked when he saw the scowl.

"No. A slight headache is all," Paine lied. He thought he looked ridiculous. No one would believe it. The disguise wouldn't wash. He reminded himself of one of those circus bears that did tricks wearing a party hat and a tutu. It was that bad. He looked like a massive, unpredictable carnivore that had lost its dignity.

"Considering that the entire ensemble came straight off the rack," the clerk chirped, circling Paine with gloating eyes that made the agent uneasy, "I must say I'm amazed. It's practically a *miracle* . . . if you'll forgive my saying so."

"Just this once," Paine responded, giving the slight gray man an ominous glance, trying on the mantle of authority that went with the outfit.

"Of course, of course. And you will be wanting the proper shoes to match?" the clerk asked respectfully.

"That's right. Solid oxfords. Thirteen wide. With steel toes . . . if possible," Paine answered. He kept studying the strange man who looked back at him. With an effort, he resisted the urge to tug at the snug collar encircling his thick neck. He knew he would have to become accustomed to it. Just as he would have to attune himself to believing in the part he was about to play in the days to come.

The mind-set was as important as the costume itself. He'd learned that soon after the Company had recruited him in Rome in the person of Walter Hapgood. An operative had to *project* the identity he or she had assumed. Even in those callow days of his youth, he had known the wisdom of that injunction. The instructors at the spy school at the Farm had drilled it into them repeatedly: If *you* don't believe your cover, why should you expect anyone *else* to?

"Steel toes?" the clerk inquired with elevated brows. "I certainly don't get many requests for them." He seemed about to add something he considered amusing before he decided to share it with someone smaller who had gentler eyes at some later time.

"I'm sure you don't. Believe it or not, even a man of peace may be obliged to kick some ass from time to time. It's a tough world out there." Paine said it without expression as he looked into the clerk's watery eyes.

"Well, you impress me as a man who could handle that. If you don't mind my saying so," the clerk replied somewhat anxiously.

"I don't mind. Do you have them?" Paine asked.

"I'll have to look, but it's just possible I do. Excuse me."

"You're excused," Paine said.

As luck would have it, the little specialty store on West Fifty-third Street did have such a pair on hand. The big black brogans were in a narrower width than Paine preferred, but he knew a cobbler in Little Italy who could stretch them enough so they wouldn't pinch.

"Will there be anything else?" the clerk finally asked.

"Just a few small items." Paine nodded toward the display case near the door.

"We have an excellent selection of whatever you have in mind," the clerk said.

He helped Paine choose the final touches required to render his disguise complete.

"I'll have the other clothes you were wearing boxed in a minute," the clerk said. Paine paid him with cash after having informed him that he would be wearing all his purchases out of the store.

"Don't bother. Throw them away. I won't be needing them anymore." Paine was watching the pedestrian traffic hurrying by on their way to lunch when he said it. He didn't see the clerk's anguished expression, but he heard the sigh that went with it. "One must not become too attached to material things," Paine said. "Remember, when the iceman calls, you'll take nothing with you to the freezer but your balls."

The clerk was speechless for a moment before he said, "Is that a loose translation of St. Paul?"

"No. It's an exact quote from Gunnery Sergeant Wallace DePugh, a spiritual man and one who commanded respect until the day he got a claymore turned around on him near Quang Tri. Is there a barbershop in the neighborhood?" Paine asked.

"Yes. Across the street and one block to the west," the clerk answered. He watched closely as Paine strode to the door and opened it. The clerk thought he'd seen such men in all varieties until that day, but this one was undoubtedly a breed of his own. Probably one of those who'd seen the light and made a 180-degree midlife change.

"You be good now," Paine said by way of farewell.

"Well, if I can't be good, I'll be careful," the clerk replied with a jaunty smile, knowing how that one went.

"No. If you can't be good, you'll go to hell. Think about it," Paine said with a nod on his way out, "and have yourself a nice day."

"You, too, Father," the clerk replied.

He wiped a sheen of sweat from his forehead as he watched the broad-shouldered black silhouette walk away toward the Hudson River.

Paine had selected the church the year before as an ideal place to lie low for a few days in the guise of a priest should the need ever arise. It had been no more than an appealing possibility at the time. He hadn't known to a certainty that he would one day make use of it. But it was a long-established habit with him to salt his savage world with emergency exits and fallout shelters ...just in case. Such fallback plans and self-evacuation procedures were as much insurance to him as spare tires and Blue Cross were to the average citizen.

Paine was as naturally inclined to giving regular thought to his continuing survival as any politician. If his personal ship ripped its guts out on an iceberg through mischance, he didn't want to be remembered as the *Titanic* of field operatives. Anyone who expected him to die quietly with a stiff upper lip and be a good sport about it had failed to consult his personality profile.

Paine had never jumped from a plane with two parachutes when he could find room for a third. It wasn't that the prospect of death frightened him. If anything, he found it darkly alluring in a way that was too elemental for him to ever hope to discover its source. It wasn't a death wish, he didn't believe, because he had always gone to so much trouble to stay alive. It was more an addiction to playing poker with the Grim Reaper. Every time the cards were dealt, he ascended to an elevated, altered state.

He'd heard the term "combat junkie" before and realized that it was probably as good a thumbnail description of his character as any. The only thing that really made him lose sleep was his dread of being taken for a fool. When his number was called, he wanted it to be the luck of the draw, not the logical result of one too many stupid moves.

Thus, when he'd heard the archdiocese was shutting down churches right and left to trim its overhead, his cunning told him to take a closer look. A few days of research and reconnaissance on one of his infrequent forays to the Big Apple had taught him all he'd needed to learn.

Like many other huge corporations that saw dark days ahead if they didn't start trimming fat, and lots of it, the Church had slated for closing all those establishments that had lost their flocks to other shepherds. Numerous such empty vessels were scattered throughout the city, usually in areas where the pervasive cancer of urban rot was well advanced. Places with bleakly familiar names like Harlem, Bedford-Stuyvesant, and South Jamaica, Queens.

Each was an increasingly isolated outpost where faith and hope were offered to people who'd lost both long before. The one Paine had chosen was trapped in the center of the dead zone that much of the South Bronx had become. It was a stately structure surrounded by a well-kept green oasis, and looked as out of place in that diseased desolation as Mother Teresa in a biker bar.

Paine had recognized the neighborhood for what it was when he'd entered it to examine the church one afternoon. It had the look and smell of a score of similar purgatories where his missions had taken him around the world. In Calcutta... Buenos Aires... Cairo... Detroit. And the parish priest who struggled single-handedly to keep the doors open and the beacon burning was familiar to him, too.

He hadn't seen the old man before, but he had observed others like him. Tough birds, each and every one. Crusty sorts who'd been fighting losing battles against impossible odds longer than many individuals had been drawing breath. Paine sensed an immediate kinship with the priest even from the distance he had maintained throughout his stay. They were both fighters in their different ways, both ferociously independent and doggedly determined. Each accepted there were certain rules they must follow no matter how intense the combat might become, precepts that could only be set aside by becoming untrue to what you were. Paine was willing to wager the priest also spent as much time warring with the hierarchy he answered to as he did feuding with anyone else.

It was the nature of giant bureaucracies to treat everyone in the organization beneath a certain level like a sentient septic tank for the mighty few at the top. Paine doubted it made much difference whether your boss was called "His Holiness" or "Her Highness" or "Mr. President." By the time the wave of excretions got down to you, they smelled pretty much the same no matter whose orifice they came from.

And Paine knew that a man who was old enough to put in for retirement, but who chose to step up to the plate each day instead, probably had plenty of passion cooking beneath the crust; the kind of benevolent blaze that warmed things up without also burning them down.

So the old priest himself was a critical factor in the equation. Paine knew the success of his plan hinged on dealing with a man who listened more to his heart than to his mind. Because the rogue's cover was as thin and subject to collapse as spring ice. If someone knowledgeable wanted to put a hole in it, he could do so with a single well-placed punch. That was an amateurish way to do business, and Paine knew it. His reputation hadn't been earned with such a sorry, sophomoric approach. Normally his covers were constructed with painstaking care and were as impenetrable as armor plate. But normality had died with Wilson in East Germany. Since then, he'd been living by nothing but his wits, a day at a time, forever on the run; shooting, of necessity, from the hip; forced to dream things up on the spur of the moment as he went along. His only real hole card was the preparations he had made in the past for the full-blown disaster that had finally arrived.

He was about to find out if his sojourn as a priest might be the ace he needed to come up with a winning hand.

As he mounted the steps to the tall double doors of the church, he knew that if the man he had judged a potential friend, Father Martin, had moved on, the chance of using St. Cecelia's as a safe harbor had probably moved on with him. Then again, the scheme might be a bust regardless of who was running the store. John Paine's familiarity with Holy Mother Church was on a par with his grasp of brain surgery. Therefore, a full-fledged impersonation of a priest was out of the question.

He wouldn't have a prayer.

Knowing that, he was only after a setting to go with his new identity. There were some roles you couldn't get away with in a vacuum, and "priest" was one of them. A priest without a church was as odd and likely to inspire questions as a clown without a circus. But it needed to be a church that was extremely short on customers, to keep the demands on his ignorance and the resulting chance of exposure as close to zero as he could arrange. And if it was one located in a barren free-fire zone where fragile friendlies were few and far between, and anything that moved was easily spotted . . . well, that was all the better.

St. Cecelia's suited Paine's needs very nicely, but if it didn't work out, there were a score of similar possibilities on his list.

It was as cool and sweet in the twilight silence he met as it was sweltering and foul on the street outside. Two different worlds. Two different value systems. Christ was worshiped in one. Crack got the lion's share of adoration in the other. Paine stood for minutes in the foyer, taking his time to adjust to the stark transition. Any church was foreign territory to him, but some took more getting used to than others. For some reason, gloomy caverns like the one that stretched to the distant altar before him always brought to mind the Dark

Ages, and tempted him to reach for the broadsword he never carried.

When he finally advanced to the next massive set of doors, doors that were propped open by way of invitation to the sanctum or whatever the main body of the church was called, Paine reminded himself again who he was supposed to be. As a priest, he was in his natural element. It would not do to conduct himself like a tomcat patrolling a rat-infested warehouse.

So he activated the circuitry that had been in place so long he couldn't recall when it wasn't there. When he did, he relaxed. Superficially, at least.

Pausing beside the first row of pews, he genuflected toward the altar and crossed himself as he did. He was on his way to his feet when someone approached him very quietly from behind.

Without willing it, another and far more powerful set of circuits leaped to life. Something much larger than a house cat hissed and coiled and extended its claws inside the new black suit. Something that longed to twist and spring and bring whoever it was down by the throat.

Father John prepared himself to pounce.

3

So he accepted the reality that had lost its place so long he couldn't recall when it wasn't there. When he did, he relaxed. Superficially at

"You must be lost," the parched voice said.

With an effort, Paine forced himself to rise to his full height before he slowly turned.

"No one ever comes here on purpose if they can help it," Father Martin continued. The wisps of white hair on top of his head were on a level with Paine's shoulders.

"I have," Paine replied, extending his hand. "I'm John O'Neill. You must be Father Martin."

"That's right," the old man said, losing his hand inside the one that grasped it. "Please call me Marty. The ceremony around here is limited pretty much to the sacraments."

Paine smiled, nodded, and let the priest have his hand back. "Business has gotten very slow around here from what I hear."

"You could say that, John. It's been me and a few other diehards for some time now. You wouldn't be an envoy from the bishop with an eviction notice, would you?" Marty cocked an eyebrow and examined Paine's face with wise, observant eyes.

"Not at all. I'm in New York on sabbatical, working on my Master's in psychology at Columbia. I've been hoping to find a church where I might be able to be of service during my stay." Paine mirrored the priest's behavior, clasping his hands in front of him, as they stood facing one another a pace apart.

"That's very thoughtful of you, John," the old man said with a smile as he wondered how Father John could spare time from his studies to devote to good deeds and why he would choose to offer them in a place where he knew they were probably not required.

"Not really," Paine answered carefully. He knew that behind the wrinkled wedge of his face, Father Martin's wheels were clicking. "The student housing they've arranged for me is little more than a closet. I wouldn't refuse better lodgings if they were offered in return for a helping hand. In fact, I don't think I'd turn them down if they were offered for nothing at all. I haven't found continuous supersonic rock music conducive of much besides indigestion."

"I see," Marty said. Then he turned and gestured for Paine to accompany him to his book-lined study in the basement at the far end of the building beneath the chancel. Once they were seated, with the wiry old man in one threadbare overstuffed chair and his guest in another just like it, the proprietor of St. Cecelia's continued, "Has anyone ever told you that you don't put out clerical vibes?" Father Martin scowled at Paine when he said it, but there was the glint of a twinkle in his eyes.

"All the time," Paine replied with a smile. "Half of my parishioners believe I'm a retired bone-breaker for the Mafia, no matter how often I deny it. How about you?" Paine's eyes darted to the black T-shirt with "Knicks" emblazoned on the chest, dropped to the faded khaki work pants, and paused for a final moment at the white Reebok high-tops that had been left fashionably and comfortably untied.

"The management gave up years ago on getting me to act my age or project the proper dignity of my exalted station. On the street I'm frequently mistaken for a numbers runner. I'm afraid I've been in the South Bronx so long that the depraved atmosphere has left its stamp on me," the priest said. There was something about the other man that he liked, but he couldn't put his finger on what it might be. It had something to do with the set of his features and the way he carried himself. There was an aura of confidence and self-possession surrounding him without any hint of the conceit that too often accompanied both.

"We all carry the marks of where we've been and what we've done, I think," Paine said.

"That's very true," the old man replied, and thought that *that* was the essence of what it was about "Father John" that didn't mesh. Father Martin had known a multitude of priests in the forty-five years he'd been one, and no matter how much they might differ, he couldn't remember one who didn't radiate a certain respect for authority. That was the one feature they all possessed in common. A priest might be prey to the hungers of the flesh; he might be self-centered and shallow, indifferent, lazy, even mentally ill; but to a man, they knew their universe was based on a chain of command that reached all the way to God Himself.

The man seated across from him, however, was as perfectly lacking in that quality as a human being could get. Which didn't mean that he acted disrespectful. To the contrary, he was courteous and conducted himself like a gentleman, but he did so out of choice rather than habit. He could turn it off whenever he chose to, and leave it off for the rest of his life without any trouble at all.

21

Which meant he wasn't a functioning member of any tightly knit organization, including the priesthood.

It was only a hunch, but it was a strong one. Though "O'Neill" or whoever he was didn't remind Marty of a priest, he did bring to mind certain other men with whom he'd become familiar during all the years he'd spent on the harsh turf that was his parish. Some of them were cops, others were the quarry those cops pursued. But all of them were lone wolves who lived by a ruthless code of their own choosing. None of them gave injury unless there was a need, but if they did, there was seldom a need for the injury to be repeated.

If this was such a man, what could be the purpose of such an elaborate charade? If he meant harm to him personally, the old priest was quite sure he could accomplish it without having to resort to such camouflage. Could he be in flight from something? What would it take to make such a formidable man develop such a complex stratagem to disappear? Had he run afoul of that same criminal fraternity that he had just mentioned in jest?

It was a mystery and a puzzlement, and Father Martin was intrigued. He knew he might live to regret it, but he was intrigued nonetheless. Life at St. Cecelia's had been less than an adventure in recent years. The announcement that the church would be closed was the closest Marty had come to excitement in a long, long time. Was that reason enough to not look further into Father John's credentials?

No. It was not.

Was it reason enough to give the man the shelter he desired regardless of whether his bona fides would stand up or not?

Refuge *was* a timeless tradition in the Church,

after all. And the Lord had made clear that men were to be treated as His children, irrespective of the nature and number of their sins. Even as you treat the least of your brethren, so it is that you treat me, He had said.

"Where is your home parish, by the way?" he asked.

"Topeka," Paine replied matter-of-factly, damning himself for pulling a place name out of the hat that he was barely able to locate as to state. His only hope was that he was speaking to another member of the vast throng who'd never felt, or been compelled to explore, the many wonders of Topeka.

"Yes, yes. A nice little town," Father Martin replied, which was true. "I've been there once or twice myself," the old priest added, which was true, as well.

"One occasion happened to be in the spring when the Missouri was flooding. That was something to behold. It had the whole town worried at the time." This was a lie. Unbeknownst to Marty, it was referred to in the game as a "snare." It was most unlikely that anyone in Topeka would lose sleep if the Missouri left its banks since it was located sixty miles to the east and had been there for quite some time. Having practiced his calling in Kansas City for a decade, Marty was in a position to know. That was the town through which the mighty Missouri flowed. It was one of its tributaries that meandered through Topeka, a branch named the Kansas River, appropriately enough.

Having little choice under the circumstances, John Paine simply leaped into the snare with both feet. "It doesn't happen often, thank heaven, but when it does, it certainly gets everyone's attention," he said.

So much for that portion of his cover.

Father Martin was impressed by how convincingly the man lied. He acted like an individual who had a certain amount of experience at doing so. Perhaps more than that.

"I really doubt that I would need you to act in a priestly capacity. Not with a congregation that has dwindled to two rows of pews if they're willing to squeeze together a bit. It's not much of a struggle keeping up with it," the old man said with a heartfelt sigh. "Once in a great while, parents will bring a child in for extreme unction. I might need assistance for one of those. That's the only possibility I can think of."

That was another casual little snare. Any parent whose child needed extreme unction was unlikely to bring him or her to the church for the sacrament to be administered since it was only given to someone on the verge of death.

"I'll be happy to help in any way I can," Father John replied.

When he did, the ruination of his cover was complete. As Paine had assumed, it hadn't been all that difficult.

Who is this man, the priest asked himself, and why am I about to ask him to move in and share the rectory with me? He had no answer for the first question, but creeping senility seemed to handle the second one only too well.

"A priest? You? You're having me on, right?" Kevin Cunningham's tone was as incredulous as the question itself.

"What's so strange about it?" John Paine asked. "I've sent enough people into the Hereafter that I should have an inside track on the spirit world."

"I've got no argument with that, compadre. You've probably populated an entire suburb somewhere with spooks, but I don't think any of the folks you helped on their way went to be with Jesus, if you know what I mean," Cunningham said.

"You think they all went in the other direction and that's where all my cosmic connections hang out?" Paine asked.

"That's the way it stacks up, John."

"In hell."

"Precisely. And I doubt even one of them is waiting for the chance to do you a favor," Cunningham said.

"Maybe I'm working for the wrong side," Paine said.

"There's a whole bunch of people in Langley who couldn't agree with you more."

"Be sure to give them my thanks for their support," Paine said.

"No problem. But what will I do about the Pope?" Cunningham asked.

"You mean I have to worry about him now, too?"

"No. I don't think so, at least. I was just wondering what I should do when the guy drops dead after he finds out you joined his outfit," Cunningham said.

"If the guy can't take a joke, he's on his own," Paine said.

"That's a bad attitude, John."

"You hang out in my new neighborhood for a while and see what happens to your outlook. Why don't you tell me something that will cheer me up, like who the KGB's man is in the Company," Paine said.

"I wish I could, John. I really do. Rafferty's still digging through the files like a badger looking for leads, but so far the word is he hasn't come up with much," Cunningham said.

George Rafferty was master of all the information the Central Intelligence Agency possessed, second only in the power he wielded to the Director, Lucian Brock, himself. Ever since the morning his guards had found the dummy bomb Paine had planted beneath his car in the garage adjoining his palatial home, Rafferty had exhibited a certain eagerness to find the mole, if one existed, among the Company's ranks. Paine had included a message with the "bomb." It said, in effect, you're alive because I'm not the bloodthirsty turncoat you take me to be, but such a person does exist and he is likely to eventually destroy all of us if you don't get off your butt and help me to dig him out of his hole.

Being no one's fool, Rafferty had taken Paine's advice, and when a man of his kind got off his butt, he did so with a vengeance. Thus far, however, to no avail.

It was early Tuesday evening. They were communicating via public phones, according to one of their continuing, and continuously changing, previous agreements. Paine was waiting at the designated time at a booth in front of a delicatessen in Brooklyn when Cunningham placed the call from a service station in Arlington, Virginia. At such times Cunningham was reminded of the guile in Paine's suggestion that he do his best to put some apparent distance between them at Langley.

He was still being followed everywhere by a pair of Berghold's bloodhounds from Internal Security. It had been that way since soon after his friend Paine's loyalty had come under suspicion. But since his recent "confession" to Berghold of his loss of faith in Paine's innocence, the surveillance had become significantly more relaxed. Now the constant tail on him operated in the open, and were referred to as "guards." They accompanied him everywhere, allegedly to protect him from an outburst of the rogue's unpredictable psychopathic wrath.

And though they were still more concerned about his reliability than his survival, Cunningham had noted that his watchers now approached the job as little more than another routine and tiresome chore. Had it been otherwise, contact between himself and Paine would have remained as perilous and problematic as it was before. If Cunningham had plugged several dollars' worth of change into a phone beside the road, someone from Internal Security would have investigated the call.

And his surveillance would have listened in by using the latest in eavesdropping technology. With the advent of computerized scanning-laser microphones, Cunningham's portion of the conversation could have been overheard by simply monitoring its "reflection" on the closest window.

As it was, however, the two agents in the gray sedan that had been with him all day simply pulled over to the curb near the service station and waited for Cunningham to make his call. John Paine had been right. It had only been necessary to convincingly "switch sides" to make functioning as his friend's "inside man" a much safer and easier task.

"Well, if anyone can turn up something incriminating, it's Rafferty," Paine said.

"Something's going to break for you, and soon, John. I'm sure of it. Since I'm on my own for a while, I'll be able to apply myself more to do whatever I can for you," Cunningham said.

"On your own for a while? What's up? Did Jenny finally burn out on all the beatings and twisted sex?" Paine asked. He felt free to make light of

27

Kevin's marriage, knowing it to be as solid and mutually satisfying as it was.

"No. She's still soaking up the abuse like a real trooper. It's the new job. The Institute has transferred her temporarily to its London branch. Her boss wants her to learn all she can about the U.K.'s view of what's been going on in the USSR and Central Europe," Cunningham said.

Jenny had resigned from her professorship at George Washington University to take a position with the Institute for Democratic Policy, a prestigious think tank located near Capitol Hill. They had offered her a salary that was more than double what her teaching position provided, with the prospect of regular raises, promotions, and the opportunity for study abroad.

The last aspect had been the only fly in the ointment. As much as the brilliant and appealing historian and political scientist enjoyed foreign travel, she loved Kevin too much to care for doing so at length alone. No opportunity was without its flaws, however, they both realized, and this one had increased their income to the point where they could buy the house they wanted and, hopefully, leave apartment living forever behind.

"So you're going to be living on fast food for a few weeks, is that it?" Paine said.

"At least that. Maybe longer," Cunningham responded. He didn't sound charmed at the prospect. "How long do you plan to be playing priest at the church?"

"As long as it works, partner. The proprietor is a good man, Father Martin. I'll be doing all I can to make sure he doesn't get burned by giving me a place to lie low for a while, but I intend to hang on here as long as I can. It's a good base to operate from, and I have a few offensive moves in mind that will require one," Paine said.

"You aren't going to do anything else I'll regret, are you, John?" Cunningham asked dubiously.

"Nothing that any other crazed killer wouldn't do. In the meantime, don't forget to keep your head down. When the bomb goes off, it doesn't care who it hits, okay?" Paine said.

"I'm getting my wheelchair bulletproofed this week," Cunningham replied.

"And none too soon. If you're going to be cooking for yourself, I'd stock up on antacids, too, just to be safe," Paine said.

"You got any other suggestions you think might help me out, bro?" Cunningham sounded less than intrigued.

Paine did, but it required some obscene contortions that Cunningham would have had trouble with even before he stepped on the mine, so Cunningham declined, and thanked him all the same.

4

Kevin Cunningham thought he would have the bed all to himself that night with his Jenny so far away. He was not prepared for the woman who came to him as he slept. Her skin was dark, her hair as black as death, as were her eyes.

He'd shared many things about his past with his wife. Not all of them had been easy to reveal. He'd told her almost everything about the war, including acts of which he was ashamed. He'd been frank about how harrowing his rehabilitation had been, made all the more agonizing by the scorn so many had been eager to cast like stones his way.

He'd spoken with admiration and affection of the woman, too, explaining to Jenny how they had come together as if by some special destiny at the perfect moment when he was eager as a child to start a new life, but needed some loving guidance to get it launched. That was what the woman had done for him. She'd believed in him and helped him to regain the belief in himself that seemed to have been amputated along with both legs and his fine right arm. At the time, there had seemed no end to what she knew: about books, about life, about him, about love.

By the time Kevin had shared all he was willing to share about the woman with Jenny, she, too, felt love for the way the woman had taken Kevin and his life into her wise and gentle hands. There was no way her importance to his future could be overstated. Because of her, he'd found himself; come to terms with the war and what it had done to him; understood what he wanted to do with the rest of his life; redefined and reconsidered many things about which he'd been mistaken in his youth; identified his academic and intellectual strengths and followed them to a Ph.D. at Johns Hopkins under the tutelage of the renowned Sylvester Wolman, and soon thereafter into the CIA.

All these things he'd shared with Jenny, but he'd neglected to include that Sophie Ostrowsky had been his lover, too. In part, this was because she had been old enough to be his mother at the time. A little older even than that, perhaps, if the truth be told, though she had carried every year with amazing grace and he had never dared to broach the subject of her age.

Beyond that, there were simply some things that were too intimate to disclose. Kevin thought, too, that there were occasions when ignorance, if not bliss, was at least far easier to live with than certain kinds of knowledge. He knew that might be no more than a handy rationalization of his taste for secrecy, but he feared for Jenny's happiness if he told her all of it. And, since her happiness was his, he settled for knowing it was not a lie to fail to tell absolutely everything.

He'd been awed by Sophie from the first time their eyes had met. She had been a first in many ways for him: the first woman he'd known whose intellect so obviously dwarfed his own; the first attractive female to view his butchered body with acceptance instead of embarrassed horror; the first teacher to be impressed by his intelligence and eager to show him how to make it expand; the first academic to not treat him like he bore the mark of Cain for having been a combat soldier in the war.

She had taken him under her wing at first, seeing a potential in him that he could not see himself. Then, after they'd spent a year growing inexorably closer, she'd joined him in his bed. That was another first; the first woman to make love to him since nearly half of his physical self had been removed. Only then had he found the courage to admit how powerfully he'd been drawn to her all along; to the musical Polish cadence and lilt of her speech, to her warmth and wit, to a face and figure that would have done credit to any woman half her age.

And, to Kevin's astonishment, she'd responded in a way that was much the same, telling him that he was more a man with three-quarters of his limbs removed than were most of them who still possessed all that he had lost, that he was all the more appealing for his youth and even for his tragedy than so many whom others might deem more appropriate mates for her. She seemed utterly untroubled that their liaison was adulterous, as well. Kevin had decided very quickly that if it didn't bother her, it most assuredly wouldn't be a problem for him. No more of a problem than the pictures he had seen so many times on her office desk of some of her children posing with children of their own.

Their affair had continued for almost two years, during which they made love a minimum of once each week, and he had found Sophie Ostrowsky as gifted and erudite an instructor in the bedroom as she ever was before a class. Every ounce as knowing and imaginative and enthusiastic. His response to *those* lessons had also been as avid and attentive as his approach to all she had to teach him about the way politics worked on a global scale.

Year after year, she had taught and he had learned until the time came when he met Jenny while both were pursuing their graduate work. By then Kevin had already become Wolman's protégé and was well on his way toward becoming the man that he would be. In retrospect, his parting with Sophie had been as easy and natural as their joining had been. Steadily the distance between them had grown until they were once again teacher and pupil as they had been at the start.

But Kevin always knew that his identity as a man and the direction of his life were in large part the result of the woman's influence on him. Thus, he thought of her consciously with respect and even reverence. But in his dreams she was all gasps and running sweat, hissing hot obscenities to assure him nothing he could ask would ever be as wanton as she wanted and would help him to be.

How did a man tell his wife that someone's grandmother had made him as talented and tormenting in the sack as she had found him? How could he admit that much of what he felt and thought about everything had Sophie's signature at the bottom? Kevin Cunningham did not know. What he did know was that when the dreams came, they always came as a seductive surprise, and were so real and so uninhibited that he awoke feeling guilty and tangibly unfaithful.

Therefore, when he was nudged to consciousness and driven from the dream, Kevin's first sensation was one of relief that, for once, he and

Sophie Ostrowsky had not indulged in another ménage à trois with his wife.

His second sensation, however, was nothing other than cold, stark fear. Because he found he had been pulled from the grasp of one wicked woman into that of another, equally dark, equally European, and irresistible in certain ways of her own. But this one hadn't come to his bed for carnal knowledge; this one had something even more primitive on her mind.

"Wake up, you crippled freak," Martina Vlota snarled. "The time has come for you to die."

That same night, Walter Hapgood knelt in a cathedral in Washington, D.C., beseeching the Virgin Mary to lend him some badly needed help. Since his recent transfer back to the States from Rome, Hapgood had been waiting fearfully for the ax to drop. He was, after all, the man who had recruited John Paine.

The hour was late, and Hapgood had the candlelit Gothic grandeur mainly to himself. In a block-long nave capable of seating six hundred comfortably, there was only a scattering of other silent and widely spaced suppliants. Here and there, the occasional priest drifted shadowlike past the altar and along the aisles that flanked the ranks of pews on either side.

Between prayers, Hapgood availed himself of the solitude to meditate. What was to become of him, his wife, and children now? he wondered. He had served his masters faithfully all his life, always believing that to do so was right, and that he would be properly rewarded in the end.

But John Paine had managed to place all of that in doubt.

John Paine. Hapgood had always thought of it as a name to conjure with. And well he might.

Paine had been something of a legend even before he agreed to join the Company's ranks. His bloody (some said barbarous) and nerveless exploits during the war had assured him of that.

Hapgood would not have chosen to recruit Paine personally if the decision had been left to him. They were too vastly different in the way they were composed. Hapgood was programmed to do as he was told. He was capable of independent action if he had no other viable choice, but he preferred being given detailed instructions that were to be scrupulously observed. He didn't like to draw attention to himself. Working anonymously and invisibly in the background was the style at which he excelled.

Paine was diametrically designed. The man had never received an order he didn't feel free to interpret as he chose. He seemed to gravitate instinctively to the center of every stage. And the man's autonomy was matched only by his penchant for ruthless violence.

Hapgood was better at directing others to carry out wetwork assignments than at doing such deeds with his own hands. But in spite of their polar differences, the recruiter and his recruit had remained friends of sorts throughout the years. Hapgood was never very sure what the Company's roving hatchetman thought of him. Paine was not the kind of man to broadcast his feelings about much of anything. Hapgood, for his part, regarded Paine with uneasy, if affectionate, awe.

Lately, the unease and the awe remained, but the affection was history. Paine's plunge from grace was threatening to destroy Hapgood's carefully constructed career, at the very least. It was even within the realm of possibility, given the worst-case scenario when the scent of treason had men like Brock and Berghold and even Rafferty in a feeding frenzy, that it might get him "maximally demoted," as the saying went.

There was only one course of action through which he might redeem himself, Hapgood knew. It would mean paying due respect to one of the game's oldest and most honored traditions. That was the one that specified that when an agent went bad, there was no one more ideally situated to play the Judas goat and generally engineer his extermination than his recruiter.

"Is something troubling you, my son?" A too-familiar voice spoke softly to Hapgood from directly behind his right shoulder. Hapgood gasped as he felt his body being seized and hauled back to a seat on the pew, irresistibly but without excessive force.

"John!" As he turned toward Paine, Hapgood was already more than adequately disturbed at the sudden appearance of the man whose elimination had been running through his mind. When he saw the circular white collar, the black coat and shirt, the cross dangling from a chain around the thick neck, he was rendered momentarily speechless.

"*Father* John, Walter, if you don't mind. Long time no see, right?" Paine said. He took note of the changes in his recruiter since he had seen him last in Rome. Hapgood had acquired more than a few surplus pounds. His seersucker sport coat looked like it was losing the fight to contain his midsection. His bald spot seemed to be gaining ground, as well. The older man's face was puffy, and the usual bags beneath his eyes had grown into trunks. "You look terrible, Walter. Too much booze and cholesterol and stress," Paine added with a concerned shake of his head.

"Is that all you have to say?" Hapgood sputtered, barely managing to keep his voice reverently subdued.

"No. There's more, but now is not the time, and this is not the place for me to say it. I just wanted to let you know that we need to talk. Maybe if we put our heads together, we can figure out who's behind what's been happening," Paine said.

"Sure, John," Hapgood replied as he regained some of his composure. "I was thinking about you just a moment ago, as a matter of fact, wondering what I could do to be of assistance."

"I'll bet you **were**, Walter. You've always been a real thoughtful **guy**," Paine said.

"I see you've finally gotten the faith," Hapgood said.

"Yeah. You might call it a battlefield conversion. There's no atheists in foxholes, and so on," Paine said.

"Better late than never," Hapgood replied. "When and where do you want to meet?"

"I'll let you know, Walter. Don't expect much notice. My schedule is rather unpredictable these days," Paine said.

"We'll have to be very careful, John. I'm sure I'm under suspicion for having recruited you." Hapgood adjusted his position until he was nearly facing Paine, with one arm hooked over the back of the pew.

"I imagine you are, and I'm sorry about that," Paine said. "Believe me, I would have avoided the whole thing if I'd seen it coming."

"I know that," Hapgood said, "You don't have to reassure me. I'm the guy who brought you in, remember?"

"I remember," Paine answered with a nod.

"I've never believed all the lies about your switching sides or going independent, John. I've known you too long to doubt your loyalty," Hapgood said. Listening to himself, he thought he was using the correct note of solemn sincerity without overplaying it. He knew Paine had a paranoid's gift for catching the slightest whiff of deceit on the breeze.

"I appreciate your confidence. Now I'll let you get back to your devotions, and I'll get back to mine. I'll be in touch," Paine said. Before Hapgood could respond, the large black figure rose, stepped out into the aisle, genuflected toward the altar, turned, and strode silently away.

As Walter Hapgood watched him walk back toward the night from which he came, he smiled and thanked the Blessed Virgin for such a prompt and forthright answer to his prayers.

Kevin Cunningham was not afraid to die. He couldn't speak for everyone who had been as maimed as he had been, but he doubted anyone in a comparable condition would be afraid to die, either. He wanted to live, cherishing the life that he and Jenny shared together, but the fact was, when death came to him, it would come as more of a blessing than it was for many.

Thus, once the initial shock of awakening to Vlota's presence was past, his main concern was not letting her see how eager he was to kill her. Her advantage over him was considerable. He needed all the leverage he could get. Above all, what he needed was surprize.

"What do you want from me?" he asked, injecting a tremor of terror into his voice.

The assassin for the Albanian secret service was clad in snug black leather. A black silk scarf was tied tight over her head, starting just above her brows. With one booted foot remaining planted on the floor, she rested a knee on the mattress beside him. Regardless of her advantage, she had the automatic in her hand. Vlota was getting better at showing respect to all of her opponents.

"Where is your friend Paine? Tell me how to find him and I will not harm you," she said.

"I don't know where he is! I swear to god!" Cunningham began to hyperventilate consciously for Vlota's benefit. She'd chosen to leave the lights off in the room, and for that he was grateful. All he had going for him was his powerful left arm, the one he had developed obsessively until it was stronger than both arms of the average man. In the darkness she was unlikely to appreciate the threat it presented until it was too late. Kevin knew, however, he could hope for no more than one chance to bring it into play. If he blew it, he could trust that Vlota would never give him another.

"Then this is going to be a very long and unhappy night for you, I think." Vlota ripped back the covers with her free hand to get a better look at him. The illumination that filtered through the curtains from the yard and streetlights nearby enabled her to see him well enough, but brighter would have been better. It was a shame to have such a fine opportunity for sport and not be able to take full advantage of it.

But she had seen the CIA stooges parked in their sedan in front of the house. Vlota had considered making a play for both of them, and believed she could have handled it with a little luck, but if anything went wrong, she would have lost Cunningham, who was her only immediate link to Paine. So she opted for skirting them instead and doing nothing to attract their attention while she was inside with the cripple.

"You have already suffered so much," she said as she studied his stumps. "Why do you want to suffer now some more?"

"I don't! Believe me. It's just that he never tells me anything. I'd help you if I could," Cunningham whined.

"You're lying. You are a good friend to him. Let me show you how much your loyalty is going to cost." She extended her free hand across her body to reach one of several items she had deposited at the foot of the bed when she first entered the room. When the hand returned, it held an ice pick, which she held close enough to Kevin's face so he could get a good look at it in the gloom. "I found this in your kitchen. It is very useful for a number of things, including interrogation. If you think your buddies outside will save you, you are mistaken. I will tape your mouth shut before I begin, and I will not give you a chance to speak again until I am sure you have changed your mind. That will not be for a long time. It will be very bad for you and very good for me. Let me show you the other tools I found," Vlota said.

One at a time, she displayed them: a butane lighter, a filleting knife, a corkscrew, a claw hammer, a pair of pliers.

Kevin kept waiting for her to point the stubby handgun at something besides him, but she would not. He was becoming desperate. Paine had assured him that Martina Vlota loved to inflict agony. She was a genuine sadist. Once such a psychotic got started, the person frequently warped out of reality for a while. She might forget about the answers she was seeking, too high on his torment to care for anything but making it last. Then he would buy it in the worst way a man could. He realized he wasn't willing to do that to keep Paine's location from her.

When she picked up the roll of adhesive tape, tugged a length of it loose, and leaned forward to apply it to his mouth, she said, "First I will castrate you as a token of my sincerity."

"He's staying at St. Cecelia's in the South Bronx, posing as a priest," Kevin said, and that stopped her. Then his torso started to twitch convulsively, and he moaned, "Oh, God! I'm going to be sick!" He lurched up, making as if to vomit volcanically into her face, and Vlota jerked back reflexively in revulsion. When she did, the muzzle of the Heckler and Koch elevated, and that was all the opening he needed.

His left hand shot out and closed around the gun and the hand that held it. He had taken her by surprise just as he had hoped. Before she could react, he wrenched the nine-millimeter from her grasp with one savage twist. Then he whipped the butt against the side of her face, stunning her, forcing her to lose her balance and stagger back away from the bed before she tripped and fell into the darkness that cloaked the floor.

Kevin Cunningham was grinning like a loon when he swiftly but carefully set the gun down for an instant, seized it by the grip, raised it, and opened fire on the place where Vlota had fallen a moment before to the floor.

Six times in quick succession he squeezed the trigger, shaking the room around him with each high-velocity sonic boom. Then he stopped, hoping she lay bleeding from several large holes a few impenetrable feet away.

"Who are you going to castrate now, bitch? It wasn't quite as easy to kill a crip as you thought, was it?" He roared his triumph at her, but held the gun at the ready, saving whatever rounds were left all the same. It was no time to be acting goofy. Not until he was dead certain that she was certainly dead.

His guards didn't waste precious time knocking on his front door. The two men hit it with their shoulders simultaneously at a run, and when they did, Martina Vlota slithered out from beneath the bed, where she had taken cover, poised her lithe frame for a moment, then plunged headfirst through the nearest window. She was on her way through it before the startled Cunningham had time to aim. It was the only time Kevin could recall cursing the fact that he'd chosen a single-story ranch-style home because of the wheelchair. Had she dived from a second floor, he knew, there was a good chance she would have at least crippled herself when she hit the ground.

"Drop it!" Both agents lunged through the door into the bedroom with guns drawn at once.

"Don't shoot me, you bastards! She's out there!" Kevin gestured toward the yard with a jerk of his head. "What's the deal? Do I have to do *all* your work for you?"

"No, sir!" Then they were gone, but so was she.

After they left, Cunningham sat there, knowing he was shaking, but ignorant of the fact that he was still gripping the H & K tightly and grinning like a hungry shark.

5

The next day at CIA headquarters in Langley, Virginia, Walter Hapgood wasted no time in his effort to relieve the Paine that had recently become so acute. Although he had fallen into disfavor due to his association with the infamous rogue, he still was a senior member of the organization, and with such seniority went a certain amount of power. And whatever Hapgood's limits might be in hand-to-hand combat, he was a black belt when it came to lethal moves of a bureaucratic nature. He knew exactly how much clout he had and how to apply it to the greatest effect.

Morgan Hill was the first specialist he summoned to his office for a talk about the assignment of neutralizing Paine. Hill was a natural choice since he was generally considered the pretender to the bloody throne Paine had until recently occupied with the Company. When Hill arrived, he was wearing one of the immaculate Savile Row suits that he preferred. With his closely styled gray hair, his Rolex, and his subdued arrogance, he could as easily have been one of the fast-track attorneys with which the Washington vicinity was overrun.

"No, thanks. I'd rather retire," Hill said, once

he was clear on what they were discussing. He looked into Hapgood's eyes across the desk unflinchingly like a man convinced of the wisdom of his decision.

"What's the matter? Don't you think you can take him?" Hapgood asked moderately. He hadn't expected such a prompt and immediate refusal from a killer of Hill's stature. Hapgood found it disconcerting, a bad omen for the fate of the small, quiet, and independent operation he had in mind.

Hill turned his attention to the window for long moments before he replied. It was evident that he was in no hurry. Hapgood assumed it was Hill's way of asserting his macho insolence without deviating from the flawless cool upon which he prided himself. Finally he sighed and returned his attention to Hapgood like a long-suffering parent who must again elaborate on the proper employment of a prophylactic to a slow and accident-prone child.

"If you think you can sway me by a lame attempt to ignite my latent fears of my own inadequacy, you are wasting both your time and mine, Hapgood," he replied. His use of the surname was his way of underscoring that he might feel obliged to pay attention, but he wasn't about to fawn. "I've proven myself too many times for that to work. What about you? How do you think *you* would fare in the arena with Paine?"

"Sanctions are not my area of expertise, Hill. They are yours," Hapgood replied. He forced himself to sit back in the swivel chair and try to look as relaxed about the matter as the tanned and fit-appearing Hill.

"That's right. I'm something of an authority. That's why I'm not interested. I believe you will find that the rest of the varsity team is of a similar opinion. I frankly don't know for sure if I could

44

take him, and neither do they. As the saying goes, on any given occasion anyone can beat anyone if the stars are all arranged in the proper constellations. But men and women like us don't survive by crossing our fingers and hoping the target will be having a bad day. We are realists and pragmatists, or we are worm food before too long.

"It's a difficult thing to explain to anyone who doesn't hunt humans as a way of life," Hill said thoughtfully as he removed a pack of unfiltered Camels from a pocket inside his coat and lit up. "We know we can't afford to indulge in adolescent foolishness because the price of failure is so high. There's no penis envy or castration anxiety or locker-room pecker measuring and muscle flexing as you might assume. If any of us have such Freudian hang-ups, we leave them with our therapist each week.

"One learns early on that you are either coldly objective or you are dead. It's that simple. I ran afoul of Paine recently in London, as I'm sure you know. It was poor judgment on my part. I only walked away because he was in an uncharacteristically charitable mood. I did not realize until then that, if anything, his reputation is more modest than he deserves." From the expression on Morgan Hill's deceptively appealing face, Hapgood could tell the assassin was remembering that wild moment when John Paine held his life in his hands, then decided to give it back to him.

"Paine is getting old," Hapgood offered.

"So is Jane Fonda, but I don't know anyone who would pass it up if she made them an offer," Hill said. He butted the Camel out in the ashtray next to his chair, then examined the fingers of his right hand to see if nicotine stains were visible.

Hapgood wanted to interject something authoritative into the pause, but the mention of Fonda brought to mind Raquel Welch, which, in turn, led him to picture Susan Sarandon and Catherine Deneuve. They were all approaching Hapgood's age, doing so with a refusal to wither that was almost unseemly, and managing to somehow become more delectable with each passing year. The potential for comparison to Paine and *his* unique gifts did not comfort his recruiter in the least.

"You know what's really scary about John?" Hill asked. He looked as if the revelation had just come to him. "He doesn't believe he's as good as he is. If he did, I might be willing to take another crack at him, but he doesn't. It's not in him. That's why I don't think you'll find any veterans who care to try him. The man *worries* about not being good enough all the time. That's why he never loses his edge. It's his self-doubts that make him so deadly. He's like the Avis of the sanction trade. No matter how often he succeeds, he believes he's out of business unless he always tries harder. If the Company could grasp that, everyone would probably call it quits," Hill concluded.

"I hardly expected you to act as his cheering section," Hapgood responded bleakly.

"I believe in giving credit where credit is due. That's why I've never jumped into a shredder and probably never will," Hill said.

"Some say with age comes overcaution," Hapgood said.

"There you go again, Hapgood. Save that crap about cowardice for the young and dumb, the ones who line up with big grins and their thumbs up their butts whenever war is declared like they were on their way to a Boy Scout jamboree," Hill said with the first traces of disgust showing through. "That's what you're going to do, isn't it?"

"I don't know what you mean." Hapgood feigned ignorance, but he realized Hill was able to follow the logic of the thing every bit as well as he could.

"You're going to round up some eager youths if all the old hands like me turn you down. You'll play to their egos and their innocence, then serve them up to Paine as fresh meat on the off chance they might get lucky, won't you?" Hill asked.

The expression on Hapgood's face was all the answer he required.

"Do you know why bull alligators are so good at feeding themselves?" Hill inquired.

"Because they're the biggest, meanest bastards in the swamp, I imagine," Hapgood responded.

"That's only part of it," Hill said as he rose and prepared to go. "They spend most of their time just laying around soaking up the sun. After a while the other animals forget they're even around. They look and act like logs, massive and heavy and sluggish. Sometimes all you can see is their eyes sticking out of the water...watching ...for hours. But then somebody does something stupid. Like stepping on one. Then you find out what one of those leftover dinosaurs can do when their blood is up. They're fast as pythons, with teeth for miles. A really big one can grab a steer and take it for a swim," Hill said.

He was on his way to the door.

"Thanks for sharing that with me, Hill. I seldom get a chance to do any serious nature watching these days," Hapgood said.

"You know what the alligator hunters say?" Hill asked from the threshold.

"Don't step on the logs?" Hapgood replied.

"They say, you should leave the big ones alone because they are very hard to kill, and if you don't kill them, all you do is piss them off, and when they're pissed off, they're an honest-to-God handful. That's what they say, Walter, and I believe every word of it."

* * *

In the interviews that followed, Hapgood found universal agreement with Hill's disinterest in pursuing Paine. And, more than that, he found that Paine was often admired and respected as well as feared. His peers found the accusation that he was a traitor to be absurd. They had worked with him too many times and knew him too well for that. They would believe Paine had betrayed them and his country when they saw solid, irrefutable proof, and not before.

All of them, that is, except Sullivan Stith.

Stith was Paine's age, and in many ways a very similar man. He was a violent loner who had served two tours as a Marine in Vietnam. The Company had been employing his modest talents for thug jobs of one kind or another for almost twenty years. He had never distinguished himself as being more than merciless muscle who did what he was told, but like many other men of his ilk, he believed this to be a grave injustice. It never occurred to him that he might have gotten exactly what he was worth.

Therefore, as he had watched Paine rise in pay and privileges and stature over the years, he had grown to hate and envy him ever more deeply with the steady accumulation of time. To this was added the shameful memory of the night in a Yokohama bar six years before when Stith had been inspired by a full load of saki to invite Paine outside for a frank discussion of their feelings for one another. Stith had spent three days in the hospital recovering from Paine's candor, and he had nursed a fierce desire for payback ever since.

"You're the first man I've spoken to thus far who doesn't act petrified by the prospect of tracking Paine down," Hapgood told Stith honestly, but with a note of admiration that was completely false. He had no use for such bull-shouldered, pea-brained specimens, considering them preferable to men like Paine only to the extent that they were easier to manipulate and control.

"The bigger they come, the harder they fall, Mr. Hapgood. I'll puke if I hear any more of that 'mighty John Paine' garbage. I think he's got a press agent that spreads that stuff around. Personally, I'm not buying it. If you're looking for someone to take him out, you've come to the right man. When do we get started?" Stith asked.

Hapgood saw little more in Stith's small, empty eyes than brutish hostility. He was certainly not the man to do any of the thinking that would be required on the stalk. For that, some measure of intelligence was mandatory.

"Very soon," Hapgood replied, "but first the rest of the team must be assembled. I will expect you to remain available until then."

"That's no problem. I've been waiting for open season on that bastard for a long time. I'll be happy to take charge of the operation, too, sir, if you like," Stith said. He'd been making the same sort of humble offer regularly for a decade without getting any takers, but he wasn't the kind of individual to let a few hundred refusals get him down. That was an essential aspect of his charm.

"I will give it serious consideration, Stith," Hapgood said as he nodded the agent toward the door. *Just as seriously as the keepers consider handing the gorillas the keys to the zoo*, Hapgood thought.

Hapgood found Vince Strado every bit as sharp as Stith was dull. The handsome young Italian-American reminded him of a jackal, and Hapgood liked that quite a lot.

"I'm like the Marine Corps, Vince," Hapgood

said with avuncular warmth. "I'm looking for a few good men."

Strado only nodded slightly in response, but his alert black eyes never left Hapgood's face for an instant. Strado's posture in the upholstered chair that faced the desk was relaxed, but he gave the impression of being tightly coiled nonetheless.

"Do you think you are equal to the task of bringing John Paine in?" Hapgood asked.

"Yes, sir. I do," Strado answered. There was the occasional suggestion of amusement around his eyes, as if he was having fun, but was too well-bred to admit it.

Hapgood knew that Strado was considered a "comer" in the Company. He and a handful of other field operatives like himself were referred to informally as the "young guns." The label was no secret to the men to whom it was applied, and none had been known to express any complaints about it.

"Do you think he will be light work, Vince?" Hapgood asked.

"No, sir. I don't. I think whoever goes after Paine should pack a lunch," Strado replied. He flashed a sudden, brilliant smile that made him look even younger than his twenty-six years.

"You think he's good, then?" Hapgood inquired.

"No, sir. I think he's outstanding. Taking him will be a real challenge." A challenge that Strado clearly found most enticing.

"And you would like to establish once and for all that you can bag the best, is that it?" Hapgood asked.

"May I be frank with you, sir?" Strado asked. He sat forward, uncrossing his legs, and rested his elbows on his knees.

"By all means," Hapgood said.

"I don't want to insult your intelligence, Mr.

Hapgood, by telling you things you already know, but sometimes it's better to lay all the cards out up front, so people understand each other. Do you mind?" Strado said.

"Not at all. Go right ahead," Hapgood replied.

"Paine is a legend, and he has every right to be. He earned it. I've always looked up to him. So do most of the other new guys. None of us ever thought he'd turn around. But once he did, we knew the day might come when some of us might have to face him," Strado said.

Hapgood could feel the young agent's eyes boring into him. He wondered if it was possible for nothing more than prolonged eye contact to inflict brain damage. Were that the case, Hapgood suspected Vince Strado could cripple or kill with nothing more than that matched pair of gun barrels he kept trained on him.

"Some of my friends aren't too crazy about the idea," Strado continued. "There's a lot of talk about Paine having forgotten more than they will ever learn."

"I've heard a good deal of that myself, lately," Hapgood injected.

"But a few of us don't see it that way. Especially myself and my partner—" Strado was interrupted by Hapgood.

"Brad Thomas," Hapgood said thoughtfully. "I know how to do my homework."

"Yes, sir. I'm sure you do." Strado went on, "Thomas and I know Paine has a hellacious head start on us when it comes to experience. That's his main advantage. But he's getting pretty long in the tooth. There's nothing he can do about that, and it limits his performance. That's *our* advantage."

It was the line Hapgood had been trying to sell without much success throughout most of the day.

Thus, it was pleasing to hear it coming from the other side of the desk for a change. He couldn't help but wonder, however, why it was that such young men still equated middle age with decrepitude. He knew he'd been a victim of that same self-serving illusion at one time, viewing people in their midforties as well over the hill, on their way to the knitting and the whittling and the rest home, where the youngsters could come and dust them off from time to time like favored museum exhibits, but he found it not only hard to recall, but embarrassing as well.

It was doubtful that Strado could imagine that Hapgood would give much to be as old and weary as John Paine once again.

"And we think, if you discount the experience, that Paine isn't better than us. He's just been around a long time. We respect that, but we're not blown away by it." Strado paused, seeming hesitant, for a moment before he continued, "For guys like Brad and me, John Paine is like Mt. Everest. If we beat him, we've proven we're as good as we think we are. Nobody can take that from you once it's done. It puts you in a league by yourself. He's the heavyweight champ." Strado went silent, realizing he was close to running off at the mouth.

"And the two of you are looking forward to a shot at the title?" Hapgood said.

"Yes, sir. That's about it," Strado responded.

"Then consider this your lucky day, because you're about to get it," Hapgood said without a smile.

"Thank you, sir. We won't let you down," Strado said.

"I know. It's not the kind of competition where you can afford to. I'll be interviewing Thomas next. If his attitude is similar to yours, I'll be

52

discussing what I have in mind with both of you later in the day."

After he had dismissed Vince Strado, Hapgood sat there thinking about a number of things for a while. Was Paine's advantage really limited to experience as Strado assumed? Or was there more to it than that? Was he really *better*, over and above the experience? He thought of what Paine had been like in the beginning. In some ways he had been much like Strado: intense, ambitious, confident. But hadn't there been more to him than that? Something wary and feral and perhaps even "genetic" that Strado lacked. To be honest, Hapgood thought that whatever that difference was, it did exist.

But did it give him an invincible advantage? Even when he had survived long enough to be long in the tooth? Hapgood hoped not. Because if it did, Strado and Thomas might not be the only ones to pay the penalty for misjudging him. Hapgood had already decided to use himself as bait to draw the tiger into the trap. It was the only tactic he could think of to insure that his killer team would get a clean, open shot at the rogue.

Which meant that if his ingenious plan somehow went sour, Paine would know exactly who had dug the pit into which he fell. The thought alone was enough to send Hapgood in search of the Pepto.

Then there was Strado's unfortunate Everest analogy. Unfortunate, in Hapgood's opinion, because a certain battered mountain climber's quote had always stuck in his mind, impressing him as one of those aphorisms that deserved to be carved in stone. "In the battle with Everest, there are no winners, only survivors."

Why couldn't Strado have picked the Matterhorn?

6

Brad Thomas was beyond intense.

He was explosive.

As he sat tensely before Hapgood, the older man was reminded of a Doberman he'd once owned. That was what Thomas was like ... wired tight.

"We'll bring him to you in sections if you like," Thomas said. He was blowing cigarette smoke when he said it.

"That won't be necessary, Thomas. Simply killing him will be sufficient." Hapgood didn't like the way Thomas's eyes glittered. The antisocial tendencies noted in his psychological profile were easy to detect. He was the last man Hapgood would want to be marooned with after the food supply had run out.

"Do you want him debriefed first?" Thomas asked.

"No."

Thomas made a dismissive face, shrugged, and looked away, but he wondered about that. Why wouldn't Hapgood want anything that might be of value squeezed out of Paine? If the man was a traitor, they might be able to force him to divulge the identities of other traitors in the Company. Was Hapgood worried about what Paine might tell them? Maybe Hapgood wanted Paine dead to insure his silence. Stranger things had been known to happen in the game before. Thomas thought it was worth keeping in mind, despite the fact that it was essentially none of his business.

When treason was afoot, it was unwise to take anything for granted.

"Whatever you say, Mr. Hapgood. It's your party."

"You and Strado like working as a team?" Hapgood already knew the answer to that, but he wanted to keep the dialogue rolling in order to judge the man before him as well as he could. He wanted to send savages against Paine, but not psychos. Not when Hapgood's own welfare was dependent upon their success.

"Yes, sir. We've been working together since they paired us during training at the Farm. It's like a marriage, if you know what I mean. We're able to anticipate each other's moves," Thomas said, appearing somewhat uncomfortable with the comparison he had chosen for his superior.

"You needn't worry, Thomas. I don't think there's anything unnatural about your relationship," Hapgood assured him with a wintry smile. "In fact, it is your intimacy, in large part, that leads me to offer the assignment to you. The more like Siamese twins you are, the greater the likelihood of your success, in my opinion. The two of you will be working with Sullivan Stith, but his function will simply be to provide you with backup. If he becomes confused about that, you have my permission to help him understand," Hapgood said.

Thomas signaled his comprehension with a nod. They both understood Stith might come in handy for soaking up stray rounds if the team found itself in a bind. And if Stith fell prey to one of his periodic seizures of self-importance, Thomas was free to remind him of his insignificance with as much force as was required.

Although Thomas, like Strado, was of no more than average height and build, both had the lean and hungry look that went with superior strength and speed. Hapgood was sure either of them could handle Stith. Probably without breaking a sweat.

The only thing that really troubled Hapgood about Thomas was his cockiness. He was holding it in check at the moment out of deference to Hapgood's rank, but it still shone out through his bright blue eyes, the way some women beamed lust without bringing any other organs into play. The trendy haircut, gold jewelry, and capped teeth only served to reinforce the swagger that pulsated from him.

It mattered little to Hapgood if Thomas's hubris got Thomas killed. What worried him was its potential for doing the same to him.

"Do you know how Paine usually kills his opponents, Thomas?" Hapgood inquired.

It was a question for which Brad Thomas was unprepared.

"He's capable of doing it in a lot of different ways, I imagine," Thomas ventured.

"Those are matters of weapons and techniques, and they are not important. It's his strategy I'm referring to. Why is it that he always wins?" Hapgood asked.

Lacking an answer he trusted, Thomas opted for silence instead.

"He has a gift for getting people to underestimate him. It's rather uncanny when you consider all the good reasons everyone has for fearing him. But he usually manages somehow to get it done. You won't underestimate him, will you, Thomas?" The look he gave the young agent, when he asked him the question, was as baleful as he could arrange.

"No, sir, but he might underestimate me," Thomas replied.

Hapgood winced in his soul.

"You're wrong, Thomas. *He* never underestimates anyone. That's another of his gifts."

When he had the trio assembled in his office, Hapgood told them what he had in mind.

"Last night John Paine contacted me in the guise of a priest. It was obvious he had gone to some lengths to outfit himself convincingly. When you are as familiar with a man's methods as I am with Paine's, you are able to draw certain conclusions from even such limited evidence. He would not have taken such trouble with his disguise if he did not intend to take full advantage of it as a cover.

"Which means he must have found some appropriate setting in which to submerge himself as a priest. He has been running for some time now. We have seen to that. Therefore, he has not had much leisure to devote to the creation of this alternative identity," Hapgood said.

It was late, and he was exhausted. He was getting too old for such marathons. He yawned and ran both fleshy hands over his face and through his curly gray hair before he continued.

"Which means, in turn, he has been forced to find some Catholic backwater in which to hide. Someplace that has been forgotten by the mainstream of the organization, where he is less likely to be scrutinized and examined in a way that he cannot afford. He is likely to have sought out a location that is physically isolated, as well. This is characteristic of him when he feels as threatened as he does of late.

"Although Paine is among the least predictable of men, he is, nonetheless, human, and to be human means to rely on practiced patterns under stress. Accordingly, he has chosen New York City in which to lose himself because such urban jungles are an environment he understands. He might have abandoned New York since our actions against him have demonstrated we know he is there. But I doubt that. He knows full well that it avails us little to narrow down his location no further than to someplace within the boundaries of one of the largest metropolitan areas on the planet.

"So I think he is still there, impersonating a priest, in the sort of situation I have just described. Your job is to identify all the most likely places that match this description and work your way through them until you turn him up. And time is of the essence. That is Plan 'A.'

"The purpose of Paine's contact was to assure me that we would be meeting in the near future for a discussion at length of his difficulty. As his recruiter, I hold a unique position with him, a position I intend to utilize as the foundation for Plan 'B,' which will entail his termination at the time and place of our meeting. We can iron out the details for the best way to handle this in the next day or two.

"If you have any questions on 'A,' ask them now and make them brief. I'm ready to keel over, and the three of you have a flight to New York to catch tonight," Hapgood said.

"What are we supposed to do, go brace the pope of Manhattan or whatever he's called?" Sullivan Stith inquired.

Hapgood forced himself to keep his eyes on the top of his desk and count to five before he responded.

"I believe if you consult with Vince and Brad, the three of you will be able to determine the appropriate course of action under the prevailing circumstances, Stith," Hapgood said with what he considered valiant self-restraint. His temptation to criticize Stith's limp grasp of investigative procedure was aggravated by the expressions of gleeful contempt Strado and Thomas were silently and slyly tossing back and forth.

"There's always the yellow pages," Thomas suggested to Strado innocently.

"Right," Strado replied with a control worthy of Al Pacino, "and they have Traveler's Aid there, too, I think. They're a lot of help when a guy's lost."

When Thomas spoke again, it was to Hapgood, and the laughter was over. "How should we approach any of these Holy Joes who aren't interested in being helpful, sir? What are the limits on that?"

"Let's get something straight right now," Hapgood said, standing to look down on the three. "We are dealing with a potentially disastrous threat to our nation's security. Technically (and by that, Hapgood meant *legally*), we are not even authorized to conduct operations on American soil. That's the FBI's exclusive domain. But there are times like this when all other priorities must be rescinded to insure that the goal may be achieved.

"This is war. Make no mistake about it. You will be doing whatever you have to do to get what you need," Hapgood said. He knew that men like the ones to whom he was speaking understood what that meant. "You will be operating under cover. Outside of the immediate family, there are no friendlies." The Company translation of that phrase was, Anyone not a member of the intelligence community was fair game. "You will answer

59

only to me, and the only thing I care about is results. Is that clear enough?" Hapgood watched as all three nodded silently.

On their way out the door, Strado and Thomas exchanged an eloquent glance. Neither had ever participated in such an operation before. Hapgood was not only indifferent to the law of the land, he was violating the CIA's standard operating procedures, as well. It was, in effect, a little private enterprise unto itself that he was undertaking, and quite possibly one that only the four of them at Langley knew anything about.

Why was Hapgood willing to stick his neck out so far to bring Paine down? Why wasn't it enough for him that every third cop in the country was after the guy? Maybe he was just tired of all the guilt-by-association he'd been wading through. Maybe that's all there was to it.

Maybe.

Charity Brock was her doting father's pride and joy. He had given her everything. A pony when she was five. A private tutor to help her with the entrance exam to the most exclusive elementary school on the eastern seaboard. World travel. A nanny of her very own. A thoroughbred mare when Charity was ten. Riding lessons. Dancing lessons. Singing lessons. A catamaran when she was twelve. Stud service when she was fifteen... for the mare. Clothes. Cars. Carnivals. Bryn Mawr. The list was longer than Charity herself.

It could be said that he had done everything within his power to turn her into a pampered, petulant, and priggish horror by the time she was of marrying age. But Lucian Brock had failed miserably, a singular lapse for him, because Charity had blossomed by twenty-one into a gleaming example of character triumphing over the privilege from which it had sprung.

It was the consensus among the elite that the beautiful, brilliant, and generous daughter of the Director of the CIA was destined to become the first "Ms. President." Mr. and Mrs. Brock found that such a near-inevitability themselves that they had already chosen a number of ensembles to wear when Charity invited them over to the White House for dinner.

Therefore, it was only fitting when Charity was wed to the most eligible young Senator on Capitol Hill that her reception should be "the" paramount event of the Washington social season. Lucian Brock approached it the way some Hollywood directors were known to approach their cinematic extravaganzas. The preparation started a year in advance. He viewed the cost with equal parts of chagrin and pride. The eventual price tag was sure to be as historic as every other aspect of the event.

It was understood there could be only one proper location, the celestial Eastridge Yacht Club on the shore of Chesapeake Bay, where the Brocks were charter members and their sixty-foot schooner was berthed. The guest list, which was confined of necessity to only the most old and intimate and, therefore, worthy of friends, numbered slightly above six hundred.

The caterers arrived the day before to begin setting up the tents and erecting the several bandstands. The food and drink arrived at dawn the next morning in two semi tractor-trailer rigs. There were envious mutterings among some of the laborers to the effect that the whole shindig brought to mind the preparations for a Michael Jackson concert, the main difference being that "Charity's Ball," as they denominated it among themselves, was more ostentatious.

It was arguable that there were more *servants* at the Brock affair than there were *guests* at receptions among the less-than-elite. Noone bothered to count, but there were surely over one hundred of them from the look of it. There were butlers and maids and waiters and waitresses and bartenders and chefs, rent-a-cops, nannies, valets;

all of them in one kind of freshly starched uniform or another, a veritable battalion of flunkies in myriad descriptions.

All the servants were automatically ignored by the guests, who had had vast practice at looking through such people, dealing with them as automated, working wraiths.

Thus, it was without great trouble that one especially large individual was able to insinuate himself into the work force once the reception was under way. Nor was it too difficult for him to progress gradually from the periphery of the gay throng to its center, where Lucian Brock and the other true notables, including Charity Brock-Hancock and her handsome husband, Elliott, were to be found.

The DCI was at his most elegant in an up-to-the-minute tuxedo from Armani. He cut a fine figure with his tennis-court tan and his aristocratic bearing. Brock knew he was sometimes likened to Johnny Carson among his friends. He was secretly pleased by the comparison. He was doing his best to wield a similarly wicked wit when John Paine materialized beside him and inquired, "Would you care for a fresh drink, sir?"

If Lucian Brock's life flashed before his eyes at that moment, it was not apparent from the minor change in his demeanor. He simply stopped smiling and lost interest in whatever he was saying to the maid of honor, to whom he'd been speaking.

"Excuse me for a moment, would you, Melanie?" was what he said to dismiss her before he turned all of his attention to Paine. The girl flicked a curious glance up at the hulk in the rented waiter's outfit as she left. There was something about him that struck her as wrong. Perhaps it was the look on his weathered face. There was no hint of the obsequiousness that went with the job.

"My invitation must have gotten lost in the mail," Paine said. He was looking at Brock, but part of his attention was reserved for the handful of toughs from Internal Security who were roaming the festivities. He had known they would be there and had identified each of them as his first order of business when he arrived. The more numerous rental guards were of no interest to him. They were unarmed and had been hired primarily to keep drunks from urinating in plain view or puking on someone of importance.

"What do you want, Paine? What are you doing here?" Brock asked frigidly. His eyes darted constantly all around. First, to his daughter and her husband, who were holding court only a few meters away. Then, to everyone else of significance in the close vicinity. Finally, in search of any of Berghold's men who might be looked to for some violent support.

"I don't suppose you would believe it's the free food," Paine replied.

"You think you can get away with this because it's the biggest day in my daughter's life, don't you?" Brock made no effort to disguise his lethal hatred for the man who dared to taunt him with his presence on that day of days.

"I *know* I can get away with it, Brock. And what's more important is *you* know it, too." Paine lifted a drink from the silver serving tray he was carrying and raised it to his lips as he stared into the Director's eyes.

"We'll see about that," Brock said. Each word was as cold and hard as the ice in Paine's drink. He swiveled his head, looking for one of the armed agents who circulated among the crowd.

"Here," Paine said, poking Brock's midsection with the edge of the tray, "hold this for a moment. I have something to show you before you start thinking that you are in charge of this situation."

Reluctantly Brock grasped the filigreed disk, eyeing it for an instant like a dog dropping someone had somehow handed him by mistake. He watched as Paine's left hand went to the front of his coat and undid the button that held it closed.

"My God," Brock whispered when he saw the girdle of bright red sticks cinched tightly around Paine's waist. There were wires linking them together along the top. The eye in the DCI's mind filled with a hellish vision worthy of Hieronymus Bosch: bleeding body parts, screams of agony and hysteria, corpses in abundance, a reprisal of Hiroshima beneath the bright blue Maryland summer sky.

All courtesy of Mad Dog John Paine.

"Before you beckon to any of Berghold's boys, you might want to think about how loud you want this party to get," Paine suggested evenly.

"You really are insane, aren't you?" Brock said, unable to remove his gaze from the dynamite, his eyes wide, his tan several shades lighter than it was a moment before.

"Crazy enough to donate my body to Charity on the spot if you make the wrong move," Paine said. "What'll it be, Brock? Shall we liven things up around here?" Paine's hand casually slipped inside his coat.

"Calm down, John. There won't be any trouble here today if you don't want any," Brock said, swallowing his pride whole with an almost audible thump.

"I knew you were capable of reason, Brock. Despite all the evidence to the contrary of late," Paine said. The hand emerged from the coat, buttoned it, and then lowered slowly to his side. "I think I'll be on my way now. I just dropped by to pay my respects. I'm a very busy man these days.

Thanks to you." Paine finished his drink, dropped the tumbler onto the lawn, and smashed it into the grass beneath one large foot.

Some of the guests nearby were beginning to stare at the father of the bride and the waiter who towered over him.

"Why don't you get one of your minions to find the pilot of that Bell and see if he can get it fired up by the time we amble over there?" Paine prompted. On the helicopter pad several hundred yards distant from the clubhouse behind them, a sleek chopper sat silently waiting to ferry the newlyweds to Dulles International, where they would board the Concorde for the flight to Paris, where they would begin their honeymoon.

"Right," Brock replied succinctly. He gritted his teeth to contain the fury that threatened to overwhelm him at the gall the rogue was displaying. Brock beckoned to one of the hovering members of the Eastridge staff. When the man approached him, he gave him instructions that the pilot was to have his butt in the Bell in five minutes, on pain of perpetual unemployment if he failed to do so. The man looked confused for a moment, knowing the flight was not scheduled for several more hours, but when Lucian Brock snarled, "Do it!" he sprinted away toward the clubhouse.

The progress of the two men away from the gathering was noticed by one of Berghold's men as soon as they reached the fringe of the crowd. As he jogged toward them, he was barking into his two-way radio. Paine's hand closed viselike around Brock's upper arm as the guard approached to within twenty feet. He knew the guard would not open fire with the Director close by his side, and that was where Paine intended to keep him.

"Tell him to go away," Paine commanded. When

he glanced over his shoulder at the guard, the man's expression suddenly changed with the shock of recognition, and he went for his gun.

"Lose yourself!" Brock snapped. His voice was raw with all the authority he could put into it. It froze the guard in midgesture, as was intended. "And lose your friends, too! I'll handle this myself." Brock kept glaring at the man until he backed several steps, then turned to retreat into the crowd.

"Very wise," Paine said. "It's a shame you don't act that smart all the time." The two exchanged a look of animosity that was as profound as it was sincere.

"One of these days you're going to push your luck too far, Paine," Brock said. As they continued on a collision course with the aircraft, a golf cart whizzed past them on the lawn's far side. It paused by the pad only long enough for its passenger to disembark and hurry to the cockpit of the Bell before it executed a tight turnabout and scooted back the way it had come.

Paine looked at Brock and smiled. "Between the two of us, you're more likely to wake up with your head on a plate than me. I'm losing faith in using the gentle approach with you, Brock. One of these days I might decide to start wasting all the people who annoy me. If I do it in alphabetical order, you'll be right up there at the head of the line. I might get myself fitted for a Kevlar jockstrap if I were you."

Ahead of them, the Bell's engine whined and sputtered its way to life. Slowly its rotors began to turn. By the time the two men reached it, the whirling blades were a roaring blur above them.

"I wouldn't feel right about leaving without giving you some token of my affection," Paine said. He seized Brock's right hand, squirted the contents of a tube of miracle adhesive into it, then extracted a hefty canister from a pocket of his jacket. He slapped the canister into the pool of watery glue and closed the DCI's hand around it, maintaining the pressure long enough to insure a good seal. "If I see anyone following me, I'll trigger the device I've welded to you by radio control." Brock stared at the ominous tubular container, the surface of which was masked completely with numerous turnings of shiny black plastic electrician's tape. "There's no way for you to know what the range of the control is," Paine continued, "so you might want to see if *your* luck is holding today by sending someone to intercept me. Be careful with that, by the way. I don't think you can set if off just by shaking it, but I was pressed for time, so I can't be sure."

Brock stopped moving his hand and started holding it very steady.

"Maybe they won't catch me until I'm out of range. In which case I'll push the button, nothing will happen, and you will win. Then again, maybe you can get your daughter's marriage started off with a real bang." Paine grinned at Brock and gave him a playful slap on the shoulder, which made the DCI wince and glance at the canister. "I'll leave that call up to you. Now I'd say it's time to put some life into this party."

"What are you going to do?" Brock shouted.

But Paine ignored him on his way into the cockpit.

"What's going on here?" the pilot asked.

"That's a long story," Paine replied. "Maybe I can summarize it this way." He unbuttoned his coat and let it hang open.

"Don't do anything hasty, pal, okay?" the pilot appealed, understanding the summary perfectly.

"You just do as you're told, and I will remain calm, all right?" Paine asked.

"Sure thing."

"Let's go," Paine said.

"Where to?"

"Let's go over and take a closer look at the party," Paine replied.

"Are you kidding?" the pilot squeaked, "Brock will—"

"You're getting me agitated, kid," Paine said, looking into the pilot's frightened eyes.

"Okay! Okay! But my job is history," he said as he hauled back on the control and the bird rose howling into the air.

"Better your job than your ass," Paine said, "This is high enough. Now just mosey over to the shindig."

The helicopter passed twenty feet over Lucian Brock's head on its way to the festivities, lashing him with its ferocious prop wash. The sudden understanding of what Paine was about to do made him forget for a moment the black canister in his hand. It also caused him to lose his composure entirely as he bellowed every vile curse in his repertoire at the helicopter.

More than fourteen hundred eyes focused on the approaching craft and expanded as it rushed to join them. The panic did not set in until the tornadic blasts from the rotors barreled into the outskirts of the gaping throng. Then everything but the people themselves became airborne, and the stampede in a dozen different directions began. It was as if a pocket hurricane had pounced on the reception. Tents, tables, food, chairs, and everything of a lesser magnitude left the ground and remained aloft as long as the chopper continued to hover overhead. Guests ran headlong into one another, vertical guests tripped over those who were already horizontal, waiters elbowed debutantes out of their way in search of cover, maids punched yuppies they'd been serving minutes before, as the general frenzy intensified.

John Paine smiled down at the disaster he was causing, knowing it was likely to grieve Lucian Brock more than thumbscrews ever could. "What a mess," he said. "This is great fun, but there's no point in overdoing a good thing. Take us out of here."

"Where to now?" the pilot asked, gratefully lifting away with a sigh of relief.

"Anyplace around New York City will do," Paine replied.

Once the helicopter had dropped him off in Far Rockaway, Queens, he removed the girdle of railroad flares that so resembled dynamite from around his middle and tossed them in a dumpster.

It was too bad, he thought, that he wouldn't be able to inform Brock as to what their true nature was. Paine would have loved to rub it in.

As it stood, the ominous black canister would have to suffice. Who could tell? Maybe its contents would come in handy when he learned it was a can of room deodorant. There was no predicting the effect such a revelation might have on Brock's bowels.

He was, after all, under a gross amount of stress of late.

whole glasses, however, intuitive felicito, that might not always rise to assembling a cross-motive personal applies theirs than asset interpretations to the general taxes.

8

Cunningham had contacted Paine immediately to warn him that Vlota had forced him to reveal the rogue's whereabouts.

After congratulating Kevin on coming so close to putting the Albanian away, Paine had given some serious thought to pulling up stakes and moving on. But he was tired of running in general, and playing catch-me-kill-me with the vengeful Vlota in particular. So he decided to wait for her instead. As defensive positions went, St. Cecelia's was a good one. He had chosen it with the possibility of being cornered in mind.

After their initial conversation, Father Martin left "Father John" largely alone. The old priest went about his limited tasks quietly, with the reflexive familiarity that came only with decades of daily repetition. He asked little from his new assistant aside from some occasional menial chores that he was in the habit of doing himself. Father Martin never called on Paine to perform any truly priestly work, and the agent noticed this, the way he noticed Martin's casual observation of him from a distance.

The signs that the aged cleric saw through his charade were slight, but Paine's profession was based on the recognition of such small indications. All the evidence supported Paine's hunch that the proprietor of St. Cecelia's had been the right man to approach.

Despite Paine's utter lack of religious convictions himself, he found the church's towering twilight solitude cleansing and peaceful. It was eerie, too, as all such monuments to the supernatural were to him, but its strangeness was not of the hostile kind. Even the smells that permeated the place were odd to Paine. He found them not unpleasant, but difficult to identify. It was a timeless mingling of aromatic candles and faded flowers; linseed and incense; polish for the spotless stone floors; and all the bodies that had bent and breathed and sweated through some suffering throughout its maze of kneeling nooks and somber granite grottoes.

It was an atmosphere conducive to meditation, if not to prayer, and Paine took full advantage of it to purge the chaos of recent weeks from his mind. Early on, he'd discovered the most private place of all in which to indulge in some lengthy and uninterrupted thought.

Along both of the aisles that paralleled the length of the nave, several sets of what looked to Paine like freestanding closets were arranged. Though not a Catholic, he was knowledgeable enough to know that these were the confessionals. Like everything else at St. Cecelia's, at some time years before, they had all been in great demand, but now they did little more than gather dust over the ornate scrollery carved into their hardwood surfaces. Each small cubicle was provided with an upholstered seat; was fairly comfortable, if claustrophobic; and was every bit as silent as the up-ended coffin it resembled.

It was on the evening of his third day at the

church that Paine discovered the peril that even the sanctity of the confessional held in store for him. After assuring himself that he shared the church only with a Puerto Rican girl whom he could tell at a distance was not the meagerly endowed Albanian, Paine slipped silently into one of the cubicles. He had some mayhem to mull, and wasted no time getting right to it.

No more than five minutes passed, however, before he heard the door to the adjoining chamber softly open and close. Being the clever man that he was, it took the rogue no time at all to realize he was screwed.

In the midst of the partition that divided Paine's cell from the one next to it was a window of sorts. The vertically sliding panel that covered it was down, and could be raised only from his side. He suspected that the penitent who was seated mere inches away was waiting for him to "open up for business" as it were. He assumed it was the girl he had seen, and wondered if she would go away if he ignored her long enough.

The rap from the other side, which was not long in coming, answered that question in short order.

Knowing that his cover was at risk if he didn't do *something*, he raised the panel to reveal the black mesh screen that covered the opening. No more than a vague silhouette was visible through it.

"Forgive me, Father, for I have sinned. It has been six months since my last confession," the sweet, soft voice said.

John Paine grimaced in the darkness. This was no part of his plan. He understood the meaning of "sacrilege" and did not desire to violate another person's religious beliefs. He had no fear of incurring eternal damnation on himself, being the heathen that he was, but the prospect repelled him nonetheless. It struck him as a particularly low and reprehensible thing to do, a species of slimy behavior on the order of copulating with an unconscious drunk.

But what if he backed out now and refused to go any further? What would *that* do for the girl's faith? Paine couldn't say. But his gut told him that if one of them must pay the price for his pretense, it should be him and not her. Better he should have to live with having deceived her so indecently than that she should live with the painful memory of his deceit.

He comforted himself with the assurance that the girl was probably a pillar of virtue who had little if anything to confess, that it would be over quickly, and she would soon be on her way.

"I'm afraid I'm a hopeless slut, Father," she whispered.

"Pillar of virtue" was definitely out.

"I've done so many bad things, I hardly know where to start," she continued.

"Short and quick" looked extremely unlikely, as well.

"I want it all the time, Father. The only time I'm not horny is right after, but that doesn't last very long before I'm in the mood again. I know you don't know what it's like, but believe me, it can drive you crazy!" Her melodious voice was plaintive. It was clear she had a serious problem.

John Paine shook his head as he sat there taking it all in, certain that if she carried on like that much longer, he would have a serious problem of his own.

"So I'm told," he grumbled.

"I don't go looking for trouble, Father. I really don't. But a lot of guys like the way I look, and when the cute ones smile and start to follow me around . . . before you know it, they're in my pants.

Oops. I mean..." The way she cringed at her own crudeness was audible in her voice.

"I *know* what you mean, child. Go on," Paine replied. It wasn't until he reflexively swiped at the perspiration that had materialized on his forehead that he realized the temperature in the cubicle seemed to be increasing.

"I wouldn't have been so long between confessions, Father, but this is all so embarrassing... so shameful...so *exposing*. It makes me feel naked just talking about it," the girl said.

Paine groaned in spite of himself.

"What was that, Father?" she asked tenderly.

"Never mind," Paine said.

"Maybe I should go to a doctor to get some help. I don't know if something's wrong with me, or what. You know? But I don't feel like I'm sick. If all the stuff I love wasn't so sinful, I'd be doing fine, but it *is*! I've been with a dozen different guys since my last confession, and I would have been with a dozen *more* if I wasn't afraid of catching something. So I'm not just a slut. I'm a slut who's frustrated! I know how awful that is, but I can't help myself," she whimpered.

"The flesh is weak and leads us all to sin, my child," Paine intoned. He knew plenty about weakness, especially of the variety with which the penitent was afflicted. In fact, he could feel the cracks spreading through his limited supply of virtue at that very moment.

"When something gets me hot, I quit caring about anything but getting off. I've done it on park benches, in elevators, at the movie, at work, you name it," she said.

"That's a thought," Paine muttered.

"The steamy weather doesn't make it any easier, either. You can't wear much, so I run around all the time in halters and shorts, and that makes

75

me feel sexy. I'm not trying to show off. I can't help it if the Lord gave me a great body," she said, sounding quite proud and a little defensive.

"It's hard to be humble when you're perfect," Paine said, straining to remember what she'd looked like when he glanced in her direction. From the little he could recall, she might be just as delectable as she assumed.

"You're right, Father. I'm stuck on myself. That's another sin I've been committing a lot lately. Sometimes I stand in front of the mirror in my apartment with my clothes off and stare at myself until I'm turned on, especially when it's real hot and my body's all warm and sweaty." From the sound of her voice, it seemed that her remorse was rapidly fading.

"Oh, no," Paine grumbled. His clerical collar seemed to be shrinking, making it harder and harder to breathe.

"I don't have an air conditioner, so I take showers to cool off. Real *long* showers, Father," she said in a voice that was deepening perceptibly.

Paine could see what was coming and he braced himself for it like a sailor who spots a gale on the horizon.

"I like to use tons of shampoo, Father, so there's plenty of lather to spread over my breasts and my belly and down between my thighs. That isn't sinful, is it, *Father*?" She had moved her lips close to the screen so that when she exhaled the last word slowly, Paine could feel the moist warmth of her breath upon his cheek.

"The way *you* do it, it probably is," Paine replied, mopping his forehead with his black sleeve.

"I'm afraid you're right, *Father*," she sighed through the screen.

He noticed that the way she was saying "Father" had suddenly changed in such a way that it sounded suspiciously like "lover." He found himself wondering how common was this sort of confession. Maybe the priesthood was a more perilous calling than he had realized.

"Especially since I got the new shower head. It's one of those adjustable kind. You turn it one way and the water is a long, hard spike driving into you. Turn it another way, and it's like little teeth biting you all over. Or fingernails, scraping over your nipples, scratching long red lines over your butt," she said. Her voice was deeper still. She no longer seemed to be confessing so much as reminiscing or fantasizing.

If she's fantasizing, Paine thought, she's not alone.

"Do you think I'm a bad girl, Father?" she asked.

"There's no doubt about it," Paine replied sincerely.

"And I haven't even told you the worst part yet," she said.

Paine could see the way she had pressed her lips against the screen. They were good lips. No less lush and promising than he had expected.

"Maybe not, but I'll bet you're about to," he said.

"I'll stop, Father, if you think I should. What I have to say might embarrass you," she said.

"Why not get it all off your chest while you're at it?" Paine suggested, feeling less and less like Father John all the time.

"That's what I want. To share all my secrets with you. To show you *everything*," she said.

Paine could smell her excitement wafting in to fill all the small space around him through the screen. As incredible as that was, he knew it to be true. There was no other smell in his experience that was even remotely like that of a woman in heat.

"I don't think this is quite the place for *that*," he said, suddenly concerned that the girl might utterly lose control. He wanted to be no part of some debauched performance in the middle of the house of God in which he had taken sanctuary. The same performance a discreet distance from the church might, however, be a completely different proposition, so to speak.

"No. It's not, Father. You're right. But *you* are the *man*. I've wanted you from the moment I set eyes on you. I know how terrible a sin that is, but it's the truth, so at least I'm not a liar as well as a tramp. For two days now, I've thought of nothing but you! It's killing me, Father! It's tearing me apart! Help me, Father, please! What can I do?" She was all but biting the screen by then. With all due appreciation for the suffering he had caused, he still felt a little relieved that there was something solid between the two of them.

Perhaps it was the thought of something solid between the two of them that spurred Paine to regain control of the situation that had gotten so far out of hand.

"What is your name, child?"

"Chita, Father. Chita Torres. You don't hate me now, do you, Father?" Her voice was both lusty and pleading.

"No, Chita. I don't hate you, and since you've been so honest with me, I've decided to be honest with you, too," Paine said.

"Oh, thank you, Father, thank you, God bless you!"

"First, I think I know the best way to relieve your suffering," Paine said compassionately.

"Whatever you say, Father. I trust you completely," she said.

"Second, and this will have to be our little secret of the confessional, like your sins . . ."

"Yes, yes!" she said.

"I'm not really a priest, Chita," Paine said.

"*Cabrón!*" she hissed.

"Yes, that's pretty accurate," Paine replied, bracing himself to step out of the booth and learn if he had misjudged the body that went with the voice. He knew that fate was a joker that sometimes indulged in the most tasteless of practical jokes. Like giving a two-hundred-pound middle-aged woman a ninety-pound teenager's voice. But when Chita Torres steamed out of her side of the confessional, Paine decided she could be forgiven if she viewed herself as God's gift to the men of the world, because she wasn't very far from being just that.

"Not a *priest*?" The words were steam escaping from the dark beauty's quivering lips. "What the hell are you doing here if you're not a priest? You some kind of sicko or something? Is this how you get your kicks?" Her fists were balled and ready to fly as she advanced on him like a stalking cat.

Paine retreated a step, with both hands raised in a gesture of appeasement before him. "I meant no offense, lady. You caught me taking a break in there, is all. I never meant to take anyone's confession. I know I don't have the right."

"I ought to tear that suit off you right where you stand!" she hissed, looking entirely ready to carry out her threat any moment.

"I don't blame you for being pissed, okay?" Paine said soothingly. "But this is not a game. My life is at stake. Everyone but the Boy Scouts are trying to kill me. For all I know, they might have joined the mob, too."

"Wanted for what?" she asked. Her temperature seemed to have lowered a few degrees as a result of his admission.

"That's a long story," Paine replied, his eyes

dancing to the darkness around them in search of prying eyes and ears. "This is neither the time nor the place to go into it."

"Well, read my lips, sugar! This woman has the time, and she's got the place! You are going to explain it all to me, and do it nicely. You're crazy if you think you can make a fool of me . . . for *free*! "Come on, you no good bastard!" she snarled, seizing him fiercely by the arm and steering him swiftly toward the front doors. "If you can't give me absolution for my sins, then you can give me something else!"

"Is this your idea of foreplay?" Paine inquired as he hurried to keep up.

"We already did the foreplay!"

Paine laughed. "And now it's time to bare something besides your soul."

"That's right, baby. Are you complaining?" She looked up at him with onyx eyes that smoldered.

"Not at all, child. We're finally getting into a ritual that I've mastered. All I ask is be gentle, okay?" As he chuckled, Paine hoped their little scene was going unobserved by friend and foe alike.

"Not a chance, *cabrón!*" Chita Torres replied.

9

Once Chita Torres had abducted Paine, she was
not about to release him until her ransom demands were paid in full. She made clear to him
immediately that she would settle for no less than
a pound of his flesh. Neither was she shy about
specifying which particular pound she had in
mind.

While Paine was fully occupied with the task
of raising the ransom in the vixen's apartment a
few blocks from the church, his pursuers applied
themselves to laying hands on him to satisfy certain primitive desires of their own.

That same evening, Father Martin was preparing to say mass for the handful of parishioners
who still attended when he was approached by a
wizened old woman he'd not seen before. She was
attired in the Old World custom, with her face
hidden deep within the folds of an overhanging
shawl that was as plain and black as the dress
that hung to the floor. She was stooped, and she
shuffled as if the burden of age was becoming too
great for her to bear.

"The other priest, Father, the one who is so tall,
do you know where I could find him?" Her voice
was strained and dry. The brief glimpses of her

face that she allowed him left the old priest with the odd impression of ancient, wrinkled skin that framed vibrant eyes that pulsed with dark life.

"No. I believe he's gone on some errand, a mission of mercy, perhaps, to someone in need. Is there something I can do for you?" Father Martin asked. He noted that the hands that clutched the rosary and told the beads seemed surprizingly youthful for such a crone.

"Thank you, but no. Do you know when he will be back?" she asked.

"I'm afraid not. Father John has studies to which he must attend. If you have a phone, I could have him call you when he returns," he said.

The bent figure stood there in silence for a moment, as if uncertain how to proceed, before she replied, "What I have to say to him, I must say in person. I will come back tomorrow. Now I must go." She turned then, without waiting for his reply, and moved slowly and arthritically away.

Father Martin watched as she merged with the shadows, and wondered what business she might have with his mysterious guest.

Father John! Vlota snarled inside her mind. The only vow he's ever taken is to kill without remorse. I'm sure that old fool would have a stroke if he learned what that animal's studies really are. Or the true nature of the business I have with him.

Unlike Martina Vlota, Strado and Thomas lacked "inside information" on Paine's whereabouts, but they wasted no time after they arrived in New York City pursuing Hapgood's logic to their goal.

With Sullivan Stith in tow, they started by approaching the archdiocese as real estate developers who wanted to inspect any properties the

Church was preparing to auction off. The list they received was daunting, with more than thirty locations listed throughout the greater metropolitan area. Further investigation revealed quickly, however, that ten of them had been long abandoned. Another dozen could also be ruled out for a variety of reasons, the primary one being that they did not meet the requirement that the site be isolated.

Which left approximately ten prime candidates as Paine's place of refuge for them to personally examine in much the same way the Gestapo had once gone looking for Jews.

"Who are you people anyway?" the rector of St. Margaret Mary's in Brownsville, Brooklyn, demanded.

It was the third church on the list, but he was the first priest who chose to question their authority. As he was about to learn, it was not a smart move for anyone who was health-conscious to make. Father Isaac Berenson was a galvanized Roman Catholic, however, who took his calling very seriously and was protective of all those who wore the cloth. He was also, at forty-seven, a veteran of the civil rights wars of a generation before. He knew a government thug when he saw one, and he was well acquainted with his rights under the Constitution.

What he did not know so well was the nature of the three men who shared the privacy of his office with him. But that was a species of ignorance they were more than happy to cure.

"We're licensed private investigators, Father, hired by this man's family to find him and return him to the mental hospital from which he escaped," Vince Strado said, with a smile that didn't make it past his nose.

"Why does it take three of you to handle it?" Berenson asked. He was sure they were lying through their teeth. His experience with PIs was limited to Tom Selleck and Dashiell Hammett, but he knew federal muscle from personal experience. There was always an air of ruthless arrogance about them. Berenson didn't find that difficult to understand. Such men were in the habit of intimidating the kind of people who intimidated everyone else: the Hell's Angels, the Mob, any local lawmen who got in their way. Berenson had seen it all close up. They had all the power of the Pentagon or the Justice Department, or whoever it was they worked for, behind them. And they knew it. When it came to clout in the Land of Liberty, they occupied the top of the heap.

"We're Polacks, Father," Thomas said. "You know how it is. One asks the questions. One fields the answers. One figures out what they mean and tells the other two."

Stith couldn't help himself. That cracked him up. He did his best to restrain the laughter, though. Levity was not included in his job description.

"Why don't you just eyeball this picture, tell us if it rings a bell, and we'll let you get back to whipping up a new batch of holy water, or whatever it is you do," Strado said flatly. He was holding an eight-by-ten glossy of Paine, standing in front of the priest, who was resting his butt against the front of his desk. Stith was on Strado's right, Thomas on his left.

"Maybe because I'm not interested in helping you out," the priest said, crossing his arms over his chest. He was wearing a black cassock, the skirt of which covered the black slacks he wore beneath. "Maybe because if you're private investigators, I'm Miss America. And then again, maybe I'd just like you to take your nasty little fascist sideshow on down the road until you find someone who's suitably impressed."

The priest stared into Strado's shark-cold eyes to make sure he got the message that he was not about to be bullied.

When Strado's face brightened with sincere amusement and he chuckled softly, it took Berenson by surprize.

"Fascist sideshow, huh? My, my. Looks like we've got a real civil libertarian on our hands, men. You pinko peace-creeps never learn, do you? We try to be friends, and you haul out the names." Strado shook his head, gazing down at the short space of floor between them.

Brad Thomas was shaking his head, as well. He sighed with apparent disappointment before he said, "We didn't call you a mackerel-smacking turncoat kike, did we? No. But don't think it didn't cross our minds."

"Or a nigger-loving faggot, either," Stith added, matter-of-factly, "which is what you are."

"I want you goons off of Church property in five minutes," the priest said icily.

"You're not suitably impressed?" Strado asked.

"I don't want to get in any trouble, Ralph," Thomas said to Strado. "If we've only got five minutes to haul ass, maybe we should drop the small talk and get to the serious communication." He injected a theatrical note of false concern into his voice for his partner's benefit. That was the way they operated together. Both took pride in doing what they did with a certain savagely playful dramatic flair.

"You think we're goons, huh?" Stith inquired. He gave the cleric one of the meat-eating smiles in which men like himself specialized, balling his big, scarred fists as he did.

The net effect, unbeknownst to Stith, as were so many other things, was to make him look like a goon in heat.

"You're not suitably impressed," Strado recited the words as a statement this time, as if the repetition were helping him to assimilate their meaning. "I hate it when that happens. Don't you, Harvey?" he asked Thomas. "Doesn't it rub you raw when people treat you like you're not the main event?" All the time his eyes were probing into those of Berenson hypnotically, as if it was extremely important that the two should understand one another.

Berenson was beginning to realize that the trio would not leave until they were finished, and that worried him.

"It sure does, Ralph. It kicks me in my low self-esteem," Thomas said with a businesslike nod. "I much prefer people who are *highly* impressed, don't you?"

"Sure do," Strado replied. Then he showed the priest what professional skill was all about.

When Strado's kick drove Berenson's kneecap up among the ligaments that had held it in place all his life, the priest shrieked and lunged forward reflexively into Strado's waiting arms. The agent hugged him gently for a moment and whispered in his ear, "Presto chango." Then he slammed a knee up into Berenson's testicles.

The priest gagged, his face transformed to a rictus of shocked agony.

"Hold that pose," Thomas requested, taking careful aim on the uninjured knee.

"He's all yours, Harvey," Strado replied. He supported Berenson's rigid weight easily, holding him still until Thomas, who was an accomplished kickboxer, snapped a shoe into the side of the joint. The sound of the tendons popping brought a smile to his face as he gracefully danced back to land on the balls of both feet.

The priest bellowed from the new onrush of exploding torment; his leg folded under him; and Strado released him to collapse at their feet on the floor. There the man lay gagging and sobbing and jerking spastically as the three agents watched.

Doing his best to be helpful, Stith picked up a note spike from where it sat near one corner of the desk and handed it to Strado with a look that asked if he might not be able to make good use of it. Strado took it from him, giving him a knowing look and a nod, and then glanced down suggestively at their quivering victim.

"I never did have much use for guys who wear dresses," Stith said. Then he drove the toe of his shoe into Berenson's rectum hard enough to move the man's body several inches across the floor. The priest vomited as he tried to make himself even smaller than he already was, with his face pressed to his broken knees, positioned much as he had been on the morning when he had first appeared in the world that had suddenly become so barbaric and heartless to him.

"You priests like to get it in the ass, don't you?" Stith said, with his sadism showing. "So you should dig this. It'll loosen you some for whoever's been riding you these days." Stith kicked him in the same spot again. Then a third time. Doing all he could to drive the man's rectum as close to his navel as he could get it.

Berenson's eyes rolled up into his head as he lost consciousness. Strado brought him around by banging his head against the floor, using his gray hair as a handle.

"Hey, Isaac! You impressed yet?" Strado called to him. "Wake up, dude, *tempus fugit!*"

When Berenson's lids fluttered open, his eyes were glazed and crossed. Strado shook his head savagely until his vision cleared. "You see this, Jewboy?" He held the message spike a few inches from the priest's flushed face. All Berenson could manage was the weakest of nods. "I'm going to insert this first in one eye, and then in the other, unless you're ready to stop with the Bill of Rights routine. So what's the buzz? You feel helpful?"

Strado was barely able to make it out of the way in time when the priest suddenly retched again. The agent chose to interpret that gesture as one of assent. "Now look at this picture and tell me if this face looks familiar." Holding Berenson's head up by the hair, he positioned the photo directly in front of his face.

"No," he said. It was a pathetic moan.

"That's good enough for me," Strado replied, dropping the man's head back onto the floor.

"See how easy that was?" Thomas said, looking down at the priest. "And you thought we were fascists." He shook his head sadly like a man who'd been wounded deeply but was too big to not let bygones be bygones.

"I want to thank you for your cooperation, Father. You've not only aided our investigation, but provided us with a little exercise in the process. Now we have to be on our way."

Thomas and Stith walked to the door, but Strado remained standing beside the priest a moment longer. Berenson looked up at him fearfully with eyes from which tears were flowing steadily.

"Just one more thing. You've got to watch that mouth of yours. One of these days you're going to flog somebody with it who's not so nice, and then you will be in real trouble. Maybe this will help you keep it on a leash." Expertly Strado kicked the priest in the side of the head, breaking his jaw at the hinge.

Then Strado pivoted and exited with the others on his way to the next stop on the list.

10

Chita Torres stretched her sweaty body luxuriously beside him. "That was *divine!*" she moaned.

She was indeed a woman with a problem, Paine thought, as he watched the way her heavy breasts shifted fluidly with her every move. If only more women were so afflicted. He'd been with only a few like her before. He viewed them as having bigger "engines" than was the norm. Compared to the average sexually healthy female, she was a fuel-injected V–12 Jag who could outperform and outconsume all the more modestly designed competition. Regardless of any lurking anxiety from which she might suffer, Paine knew there was nothing actually "wrong" with her. No more wrong, at least, than the women who occupied the other end of the erotic spectrum.

He thought of them as the subcompacts of the sexual marketplace. Economy jobs that didn't require much in the way of maintenance. They would run forever on whatever you put in them and think nothing of it. They were built to last and to be dependable, and there was much to be said for both qualities. They were also the vehicle of choice for most drivers. One look at the road would assure one of that.

But in return for their virtues, they also had their limitations. If you were looking for a wild ride, for balls-to-the-wall, supersonic high performance, you had to look someplace else. To a woman like Chita Torres, for example. She would give you all the horsepower you could handle and then some. If you gave her her head, so to speak, she would test your ability to keep all four wheels on the road.

But she had to be approached with caution, because she was dangerous and demanding. She was volatile and unpredictable, as well. There was nothing restful about being in her company. Not with that muscular, high-pitched motor cranking to life regularly, quivering with the need for speed and burning up the fuel as fast as a man could pour it in.

Exhausting, definitely. But not restful.

She sat up and squeegeed the sweat and the long, curling black strands of hair from her forehead. Then she looked down at his brawny body speculatively. "You sure are in good shape for such an old guy."

"I sure am," Paine responded.

"You get knifed and shot a lot, don't you?"

"Every damn day, pretty near. Have you ever had anyone die on you in the sack?" Paine ran a hand lazily from the cleavage of her derriere up the soaked silk of her back to her shoulder blades.

"Not yet, but there've been some close calls. Why? You feeling suicidal?" She chuckled and her eyes darted by habit to his pound of flesh and remained there for a while, savoring the view.

Paine laughed. "Not hardly, but if I decide to end it all, I promise to let you know. You beat hell out of any other methods that come to mind." He started to get up, but Torres intercepted him before he could complete the motion.

"Where do you think you're going? Did I say you could get out of bed?" She rolled over on top of him, jamming one muscular thigh between his legs, laughing silently and enjoying her own aggression.

"Careful," Paine said, "you don't want to damage anything that's precious to both of us." He liked the warm feel of the sweat raining down from her skin onto his. He liked the rank smell with which both of them, the bed, the room, and, for all he knew, the whole building was soaked. The way she was, and the way it was with her, were the sort of things Paine understood. Not in his head so much as in his bones. Her approach to sex was similar to his approach to violence. It was something she had found a taste and talent for long before, and as she exercised her essence over time, both her skill and her tendency to put it into play increased until there were few who were her equal in that particular arena.

"Relax, stud. This girl's mama didn't raise no fools. I know what happens if you bust a tiger's balls. You end up in a tiger taco! Right?" she said. Chita squatted back on her haunches, posing for him, raising both arms to push back the obsidian cloud of her electrified hair. She knew the ripe globes of her breasts looked best when she made them stand up, jutting drastically over the sheer drop that plummeted pleasantly to the wild midnight jungle that pointed the way irresistibly to her belly's base.

Paine studied her and reacted in a predictable way, happy to give the display the response it deserved. "Is that what I am? A tiger?" he asked.

"Uh huh," she replied. "So what are you doing acting like a priest?"

"I figured I should get some religion before it's too late," Paine responded. He kneaded his way up the length of her thighs with both hands until he reached the lean swell of her hips.

"Is that why I had so much trouble dragging you up here? Because you wanted to save me from my sinful ways?"

"That's right. Call it missionary work," Paine said.

"The only *missionary* work you're into is the *missionary position*, but we haven't even gotten around to that one yet. I thought you said you were going to tell me the truth," Chita said. She leaned forward and placed one hand on each of his shoulders, paralleling her naked body over his. The fragrant damp mass of her hair cascaded down to enclose his head with hers inside a waving, frizzy shroud.

"I am," Paine replied, "and the truth is, I have to get back to the church."

Something like a premonition compelled him to return to St. Cecelia's as darkness staked its claim on the city once again, and another sultry South Bronx night began. Distant salsa drifted in to join them in the gloom of Chita's seedy flat, lending its spice to mingle with the bouquet of cheap wine, roach spray, and ancient garbage that permeated everything.

Paine felt too much like a sentry who had abandoned his post.

"Why?" she asked petulantly. "You're not even a priest."

"That's not the point. Wherever I go, trouble follows. It's not right for me to leave Father Martin on his own right now. He helped me out. I don't want him to get hurt for having done so," Paine said.

"What kind of trouble?"

"It's better for you not to know. Just believe me when I tell you that since we've gotten together, you, too, must be more careful from now on." Paine took one hot breast in each hand and squeezed until she moaned. "Have you got that?"

"Oh, yeah! I've got it," she said, chuckling deep in her chest as she moved catlike over him to lend double meaning to her words.

"Let's just do this, and then, maybe, if you ask real nice, I'll let you go," she said, then gasped as their bodies interlocked again.

"Okay, but we've got to make it a quickie, all right?"

"Whatever you say, baby. I'm your slave. You know that." She slipped into her own inimitable rhythm above him, perfectly indifferent to anything but the trance she was entering. The world beyond the boundaries of the bed ceased to exist.

"Do I?" he asked.

"You do," Chita answered. "Want to try the missionary position before we forget?"

"I'm game, but we're not going to turn this into another marathon. I'm serious," he said.

"That's real good, baby. You're serious. I'm serious. Why don't you shut up so this screwin' we're doin' will get serious, too?" She was not a woman who approached intercourse lightly, and she was always ready to make that completely clear whenever it was necessary.

"Hey! Excuse the hell out of me, all right?"

When Paine awoke, the morning of the next day was well advanced. It had not been a quickie. He cursed himself and the sleeping woman beside him for having indulged themselves like a pair of addicts who had just inherited a truckload of their favorite poison. Then again, he'd been suffering from a plenitude of tension recently, and the Puerto Rican beauty was an expert at dispensing Mother Nature's surest cure for that.

As he donned his priest garb hurriedly in her shabby, underwear-strewn living room, Paine hauled back the slide on his latest piece of artillery to make sure a load was chambered. Not that he wasn't 99 percent certain that one was. But his life was founded on never letting any less than total assurance be sufficient. And it was based on brute habit. He'd begun to engrave certain behaviors on his gray matter before some of the punks who pursued him had been conceived.

That, in John Paine's opinion, was the advantage of advancing age. You might not be as pretty, but if you paid attention, you got smarter. You learned economy; how to live your life with an absolute minimum of wasted motion. Once a man learned the wisdom of going around barriers instead of through them, he needed far less energy, so it was no burden if he had less at his disposal. Paine didn't know if, as the adage went, youth itself was wasted on the young, but he was convinced that *energy* was wasted on them. They pissed it away, each and every one. Which was probably for the best. He knew that if they ever figured out how to use it wisely, they had enough to become an even bigger problem than they already were.

The recently acquired piece was an Israeli-made .44 Magnum semiautomatic called the Desert Eagle, and at four and one-half pounds, he wagered it probably weighed as much as its namesake. The long-barreled and angular gray handgun was a hogleg by any man's standard. He would have preferred something more concealable and less cumbersome, but New York City had some of the tightest firearms restrictions in the country, so the selection of weapons he had to choose from, on relatively short notice, was somewhat restricted.

Fortunately, the local underworld was populated with individuals who were called "criminals" because they prided themselves on their ability to live outside the law. Gun bans were important to them only insofar as they served to disarm the general public, and thereby render them less of a threat.

The dapper, gold-bedecked crack dealer he'd approached several days before had assured him that the local "hardware store" was well stocked if "heavy metal," as he called it, was what Paine was looking for. Uzis, SMGs, Ingrams, MAC–10s, even Thompsons, were easy to acquire. It was a location and a business in which a man liked to be prepared when "company" was expected.

When Paine requested something less suited for wholesale slaughter, however, the young entrepreneur was less than optimistic. He was finally able to sell Paine the Desert Eagle only because his girlfriend had informed him it was taking up too much room in her purse.

Once he had assured himself that the cannon was ready to go to work if needed, Paine stuffed it into the shoulder rig between the black shirt and the black coat. It felt like a pot roast under his arm. He comforted himself with a reminder that should it turn cranky on him and malfunction, it would serve equally well as a club with which to bludgeon someone into submission.

"We know that you know where Johnny Boy can be found, old man. And *you* know that *we* know that *you* know, and so on." Brad Thomas leaned casually on his elbow, which rested on the marble slab next to Father Martin.

The four of them were gathered around the small altar in a recessed alcove at the end of one of the cryptlike chapels near the front of the church. The morning light pouring through the scarlet stained-glass window in the east wall bathed the room in the color of blood.

The old man lay on his back. He was tied securely.

"You can save yourself a lot of screaming if you would just tell us where he is," Vince Strado said from his position on the altar's other side across from his partner.

"You boys may be in the habit of lying, but I am not. I don't know where he is. However, if I *did* know, I wouldn't tell you," Martin said. He was neither afraid to die, nor to suffer. He considered himself too old to shame himself by catering to such manicured brutes. He was looking forward to kneeling before the blinding throne of his Maker, and when he did so, he did not want the sin of cowardice upon his soul. At the moment, his only true regret was that he had given "Father John" away by reacting so blatantly to the picture they had showed him.

"That's bold talk, pal," Sullivan Stith said. He stood looking down the length of the priest's body from his position next to his feet. His expression was one of contempt and infinite cynicism. "We'll see how heroic you feel after the first few broken bones."

"I'm afraid the man's right, Father," Strado said gently. "Most people, even good men like yourself, will sing like Pavarotti if you hurt them bad enough. So what's the point, huh? I'll grant that you're a tough old coot. We're all agreed on that, right, men?" He looked from Thomas to Stith for their agreement.

"He sure is," Thomas said sincerely. "Able to leap tall crosses with a single bound. He should have been Pope."

"Yeah. Right," Stith remarked reluctantly. He

was vastly tired of the antics of the two men he thought of as the "Bobbsey Twins" or "Heckle and Jeckle." He didn't find them nearly as cute as they found themselves. He also suspected they were queer for each other; if not overtly, certainly down in the belly of the beast where every man and woman's *real* character was stored. Or chained. Or, as in the case of Strado and Thomas, prancing around in eye shadow and panty hose.

"See?" Strado continued, looking into Father Martin's calm eyes. "We already think you're a regular macho menace, so why not be smart, too, and tell us?"

"How do children grow up to become men like you?" Father Martin asked the trio. "John is a brutal man. I knew that from the first. He's hard. Perhaps even a killer. But there is a basic decency in him that shines through. That's why I gave him shelter regardless of his lies about being a priest. But there is no decency in you. From what I can tell, there is hardly anything inside of you at all. You're not even corrupt."

"What are we waiting for?" Stith interjected. "I didn't come here for a sermon. Let's get on with it."

"Hold on, Sully," Thomas said, looking at Stith with blue eyes that gleamed like glacier ice. "Pay attention. You might be able to learn something. Maybe the old man's got a point. What do you think, Lester?" he asked Strado.

"I always thought we were corrupt, but I might have been wrong," Strado replied, shrugging non-committally.

"You two really get off on your little stand-up routine, don't you?" Stith inquired disgustedly, his patience at an end.

"That's right, Sully," Thomas answered. "Don't deny us what small pleasure we derive from it,

98

okay? Because we only have two pastimes we really enjoy, and the other one is crippling loud-mouthed morons. If we lose one, we'll have to start practicing the other to have a good time. Would you like a few minutes to figure out what that means? We can wait. The good Father isn't going anywhere." Thomas looked into and through Stith in a way that made the latter want to reach for the Colt in his belt holster.

Strado watched the confrontation intently, listening all the while for any telltale sounds of movement in the church outside the chamber. He knew that Stith was right. It was time to set the merriment aside and take care of the business at hand.

Just then there came to them the sound of something falling to the floor in the vicinity of the main altar at the far end of the nave. It was an open and clumsy sound, the kind made by a civilian, not a career assassin.

"Check it out, Sully," Strado said, glancing at the man, then nodding curtly in the direction of the sound. "Go on. Move it. You two can pick up where you left off later when we have more time."

With some effort, Stith broke eye contact with Thomas, and slipped quietly out into the aisle. Turning toward the altar, he followed it past the first set of confessionals, keeping his eyes fixed on the side entrance from which he guessed the noise had come.

When John Paine's steely left arm slammed into place around his neck, all Sullivan Stith could manage was "Huh?"

"Typical," Paine whispered as he dragged Stith back with him into the concealment provided by the confessionals. "You should have learned your lesson in Yokohama, Sully."

Stith kicked back with his heel, aiming for

Paine's shin and missing. The left arm pulled his head up and back savagely as Paine's right hand seized the side of his face, its heel wedging precisely into the soft flesh just beneath the corner of the jaw. Stith did not struggle to break the hold. He knew better. Instead, he rammed his right elbow back into Paine's ribs with all his strength. Then again. And again. As he heard things beginning to pop and snap in his neck. It was his only hope, and he knew it. Paine felt first one rib crack, followed closely by another. He ground his teeth together against the pain and concentrated all his strength in his arms. Breaking any man's neck was hard work. Breaking it silently was a certified challenge. Stith kicked again, and connected this time. A white bolt of pain flashed through the rogue's wiring into his brain, demanding immediate attention. Paine refused the demand. He lifted Stith into the air and the cracked ribs roared. Ferociously the left arm pulled Stith's head back farther and farther as the right hand drove the skull to the side, twisting the cervical spine. Both men's faces were sweaty and swollen from the enormous strain. Stith was turning blue and losing consciousness as the blood supply to his brain was interrupted. Paine was deep crimson. He wished it were as easy as it appeared in the movies. And he wished Stith would cooperate, but even from a fool like Stith, that was asking quite a lot. *Come on, break, you bastard!* Paine snarled quietly as he shook Stith like a great, ugly doll, levering his head ever farther back and down, trying to touch the man's ear to the blade of his left shoulder. Then, with one final wild and concerted thrust, the wet snap came, the sound a sapling might make, and Sullivan Stith's body went limp. Paine lowered him to the floor with great care, struggling to catch his breath without giving himself away.

Were it not for Father Martin, the other two were his now for the taking. They were no doubt good, however, or they would not have been sent after him. And if they were good, he could not be sure of taking them easy. Being unsure, he could not risk it. First he must draw them away from the church and its rector. Draw them off, and deal with them later, if necessary, at some safe distance. Safe, at least, for the old man who had sheltered him.

With Stith finally being cooperative, Paine made sure the job was done properly, twisting his head around completely into a position the rogue found far more appealing than the original. Then he hoisted the dead weight up into the air.

"I wonder what happened to Stith," Strado remarked.

Both agents listened closely for any hint of trouble, but heard nothing.

"Perhaps he's seen the light, young man," Father Martin said with more energy than he felt. He sensed that the two were nervous, and if the impression he'd received from "Father John" was correct, they might have every reason to be. If he could be of service to the man they sought, and to himself, by distracting them, he considered it the least he could do. "Stranger things have been known to happen in such holy places."

Strado and Thomas were glancing in his direction at the moment when John Paine appeared at the chamber's opening, toting Sullivan Stith's body in a bear hug in front of him.

Both men wheeled when the corpse hit the stone floor with a fleshy smack and the man they'd been pursuing bellowed, "Here's Johnny!"

11

Paine was gone before Strado and Thomas could get to their guns. The outrageousness of his maneuver had the desired result. It froze the two agents in place for the seconds he needed to make good his flight from the church. Neither man was entirely sure that dashing off in pursuit of the rogue was the wisest move they could make. The memento he'd left cooling on the floor at the entrance to the chamber was an eloquent reminder to both that his termination might be a bit more risky than they'd realized.

After they'd reconned the vicinity closely enough to reassure themselves that Paine was gone, they returned to the chamber and, like the good sports they were, untied Father Martin and helped him down from the altar.

"This looks like your lucky day, old man," Strado said. "That was Paine's way of letting us know he's moving on to greener pastures. Wherever that is, it won't be any place you might know about. So that lets you off the hook."

"Luck, my son?" Father Martin replied, looking wisely into Strado's eyes.

Thomas got the drift. He snorted and shook his

head. "Right. It was the left hand of God showing up right on time."

"The Lord works in mysterious ways, his trusting flock to defend," the priest said.

"Paine must have a real soft spot for you. He had his chance and let it pass," Strado said.

"I told you I sensed a decency in him that you lack," Father Martin said.

"That decent streak of his is going to get him dead," Thomas said coldly.

"To the contrary, young man. I predict that his humanity will save him, and your lack of it will be your ruin." The look of dread assurance on the priest's face made something stir uneasily in Brad Thomas's gut.

"Thanks for the forecast. Next time we need your crystal ball, we'll be in touch."

The two sauntered over to the next unavoidable item of business on the agenda, Stith's stiff, and stood looking down at it dispassionately.

"I always said he never knew if he was coming or going," Strado said.

The corpse lay on its chest, but Sullivan Stith's cobalt-colored expression of dying agony looked up at them nonetheless. His swollen tongue protruded through his savage grin.

"You sure did," Thomas intoned, "but aren't you glad we brought him along?" He glanced at his partner and smiled. "Be honest now."

"Yeah. Maybe Paine will think that we're this easy," Strado said.

"That guy is certifiable just like everybody said," Thomas replied.

"I know. I kind of like his style, don't you?" Strado asked.

Thomas's smile broadened. "He's a man I can relate to. It's going to be an honor to cash him out."

"That it is," Strado said. "You want to flip to see who calls Waste Disposal?"

"Not with these shoes on. I might hurt myself on this slick floor," Thomas said.

"You think Paine is waiting outside?" Strado asked.

"Nah. That's not the way he works. He'll back up and regroup. Look for a new hole to hide in. He's a very careful guy. Insane, but careful." Thomas rested one foot casually on Stith's rear end.

"Around here?"

"Maybe. It's worth considering," Thomas answered, staring down at Stith, whose distended eyes were staring back. "I was looking forward to killing him myself, but it's better that it turned out this way. He was a palooka who got one final shot at the top."

"Sort of like *Rocky* in reverse," Strado said, nodding.

"There's something to be said for getting yourself offed by the best," Thomas said.

"I know what it is, too," Strado replied, looking into his partner's eyes.

"I'm all ears," Thomas said.

"Better him than me."

"I'll second that motion," Thomas replied.

"I'm back," Paine said.

He was waiting for Chita Torres in her apartment that evening when she returned home from work.

"So I see. You picked all six of my locks?" Her irritation was apparent as she strolled over to the couch, where he was sprawled.

"Don't worry. They're good locks. The average hype would need a sledgehammer to get in." He watched as her long pink talons dragged the zip-

104

per down the front of her Burger King smock.

"The average hype carries one," she said. "D'you take care of your business at the church?" Chita slipped out of the smock and tossed it on the floor. The bra she wore was one of her favorites and translucent. She was happy she had chosen to wear it to work that day.

"You could say that, yes." Paine was glad she had selected it, too.

"What else could you say?" she asked.

"I got evicted," he said.

"By Father Martin?"

"No," he replied.

"You want to shack here for a few days?" She stepped out of her sneakers, opened her slacks, and let them drop before kicking them in the direction of the smock.

"Would you mind?" he asked.

Chita smiled at him, running her thumbnails between the waistband of her string bikini and the dusky satin skin to which they clung. "I guess not."

"Some people who wanted to have a talk with me were about to put a few new wrinkles in the old man when I interrupted them. They're the kind who don't care who they hurt. Senior citizens. Sexy señoritas. It's all the same to them. If you want me to park myself someplace else, I'll understand," he said. He did his best not to let his eyes drift to her pressure points, regardless of the way she looked, or the way she wasn't dressed, or the provoking way she stood, but that was a losing battle. He finally settled for refusing to drool.

"Yes, but will you respect me in the morning?" she asked. Her sweet-sinful face was half appeal, half challenge.

"Just as much as I respect you now," Paine replied. He watched the way she tugged the bikini up to make the outline of her sex more prominent. The woman, he thought, was utterly wasted on Burger King.

"Which is not at all, right?" she asked.

"Right."

"Okay. Then you can park yourself anyplace you like," she purred.

"Do you have a preference?" he asked.

"The lot's open, baby. Pick any slot that turns you on," she responded, moving closer. "And don't worry about me. I can take care of myself. I'm a barrio lady. I been dealing with guys who thought they were the worst of the bad since I was born. They come *here* and try to evict you, and maybe I feed them their *cojónes* for lunch!"

Paine picked a slot that appealed to him and parked.

He stayed with her that night and the next day, which she decided to take off from work. During that time, Torres kept his body occupied almost constantly. But his mind was busy elsewhere, focused on far less pleasant things.

Who were the two young toughs he'd caught a glimpse of in the church? That they were Company agents was a given since they'd been working with the unlamented Sullivan Stith. But were they assigned to Internal Security? Was Mark Berghold running them? Paine found that to be unlikely. Berghold believed in doing things by the book. He would know as well as anyone that Company agents were without authority in the United States. To send his men after someone who was on home ground was a felony. Berghold was too religious about covering his own ass to do something like that.

So who did they answer to? Who at Langley

wanted him bad enough to risk imprisonment to bring him down? Could it be the mole himself? Or was it *her*self? Wasn't the mole too sly to become actively involved in his termination? Or was the mole so cunning that he or she knew that such active involvement would deflect suspicion by its very obviousness? The twists and turns of all the possibilities amounted to a labyrinth of logic in which there was only one proper path and a multitude of frustrating dead ends.

How had they tracked him to the church? Who could have put them on to him? Cunningham had been forced by Vlota to disclose his hiding place, but the Albanian was conducting her one-woman vendetta completely on her own. She would never share his location with anyone, lest they cheat her of the pleasure of killing him.

Who else knew of his cover?

Walter Hapgood knew.

The more Paine thought about it, the better Hapgood sounded as a likely suspect. Still, they were friends, and friendship stood for something, even in the icy waters in which the two of them swam. Hapgood was the one who'd brought him in. The two of them had worked together repeatedly over the years. If anyone had reason to trust in his loyalty, it was Hapgood.

But what if Hapgood knew he was loyal and didn't care?

What if Hapgood himself was disloyal?

What if Hapgood was the mole?

It was possible. It was also possible that Hapgood felt a need to redeem himself from any taint of his association with his recruit by either bringing him in, or assisting someone else to do the same.

Whatever the case might be, Paine knew it would be wise to approach the upcoming meeting with Hapgood with more than the usual amount of care.

"Why don't we get you some different clothes?" Chita whispered. "People in the building are starting to talk. Most of them are P.R.s, and that means they're Catholics. You never know what they might do if enough of them think I'm doing it with a priest. They might burn me at the stake or something."

She lay at his side the next night with her head on his chest.

"I'll be leaving soon. Probably before they work themselves up to any mob violence. Anyway, I've grown fond of this cover. I don't think I'm ready to drop it yet," he replied as he absentmindedly caressed her shoulders and stared up into the darkness.

"Cover, huh? That makes you a secret agent man, doesn't it?" She dragged her fingernails lightly over the dark fluff that forested the flat plain around his navel.

Paine silently cursed himself for the slip of the tongue. "Not exactly. I work for the IRS. I'm a tax collector. That's why so many people hate me."

"I heard people say they had guys like you working for them, and I always figured they were just paranoid. But it's true, huh?" She sat up beside him, her amusement at his creative lie breaking the spell of après-sex that she'd been under. When she did, she leaned against his injured side for a moment, and he recoiled suddenly, snarling from the hot wire of pain.

"Sorry, baby!" she gasped, from his reaction as much as anything.

"That's all right. Just don't make a habit of it," he grumbled. "Why do you think people are so afraid of us?"

"You break their bones and stuff, huh?"

"To make sure they're listening. Then I really go to work on them. Want a demonstration?" He made a playful grab for her arm, missed it when she zigged, and latched on to one full breast instead. Chita laughed and made a snaking grab for something of his that was equally sensitive and equally available under the circumstances. Once she had it in hand, she said, "What was that about a demonstration?"

"Now that you've got such a handle on the situation, it sort of slips my mind," Paine said.

"I thought it might," she said. "I told you I knew how to deal with you tough dudes, didn't I?"

"That you did," he replied. "Before one thing leads to the next, you want to go somewhere for a drink?"

"With you dressed like a priest?" She did not sound charmed by the proposition.

"Sure. It might give you a whole new reputation," he said.

"How do you know I want a new one? Maybe I like the old one just fine. For all *you* know, I have a *great* reputation!" She gave him a hard squeeze and a defiant toss of her head as she said it.

"Okay, okay! You've got a great reputation. Forget about it, all right? I'll go get a drink by myself."

"I was just kidding, baby. I don't care if the whole South Bronx thinks I'm a whore who leads priests into sin. They ain't so smart anyway, or they wouldn't be living here. So let's go."

"I'm right behind you," Paine said.

"Good. That's where you do your best work," she fired over her shoulder.

* * *

Paine knew the ghetto world through which they moved, though he had never walked those specific streets before. He had, however, trod many others that were identical to them. In Mexico City, San Salvador, and Rio, among others. The only possible difference being that the South Bronx was not as bad. It was foul and desperate, yes. But it was still the U.S. of A., where dead cars might be left to rot for years, but humans were not. Paine knew that was the sort of "small" thing the average citizen took for granted if he or she'd never had the enlightening experience of visiting the *real* Third World. Without it, one could not understand that bums in America were better off than the working poor in scores of other nations.

Paine found it darkly amusing that so many of the "underprivileged" complained so loudly about conditions in his country's admitted underbelly. He knew there were lawyers in Calcutta who would find emigration to the South Bronx an exhilarating improvement in their standard of living. To them, dependable running water and electricity, plumbing that worked most of the time, and rats that were too small to force their way into your apartment qualified as luxuries that were unavailable in their native land. It was that way more often than not throughout the rest of the world. If more of his countrymen knew that, Paine believed they might be more inclined to wave the flag than to burn it.

He also found all the whining about "fascist oppression" in the land of milk and honey pretty hilarious, too. Though it was no longer the migraine-inducing din that it had been back in the sixties, there was still plenty of it going around. In Paine's opinion, Americans as a whole were so pampered, and spoiled as a consequence, that they'd totally lost touch with why half of everyone on the planet was living for the day they could move in next door. They needed to take a trip; needed it so badly that he was convinced the government should provide every citizen with one brief, all-expense-paid tour to any of a hundred other places he could think of where they took a distinctly different view of "civil rights."

Like Leningrad, where you might be arrested and held incommunicado for a year before they decided you weren't the one they were looking for in the first place. Sorry about that, comrade. These things will happen. No hard feelings, right? Or Istanbul, where you could either confess or take your chances on being crippled for life by your interrogators, who tolerated the low pay because they found such pleasure in their work. No one had ever heard of the Miranda warnings in Turkey. Or Iran. Or Bolivia. Or a whole bunch of other places.

Paine knew that anyone who thought the local badges were storm troopers had never met the genuine item. Even in relatively "civilized" settings, like Hamburg or Marseilles or Athens, if the cops hauled you "downtown" for a "chat," you were well advised to cooperate and be polite unless you yearned to have your ass kicked up above your ears, because it was all the same to them.

That was why certain American films didn't do well overseas. Films like *Dirty Harry* were confusing to audiences who had known all their lives that if the police didn't work you over, it was only because you'd caught them on a good day. All the fuss about Harry Callahan's methods were, for them, a mystery. After all, the man was just doing his job, wasn't he?

Paine saw the trio of young Hispanics loitering

on the sidewalk in their path far enough in advance to give them a good inspection. They looked like they might be trouble, but none that he couldn't handle without resort to the Desert Eagle. He'd cut his teeth on such unruly children and was concerned only for Chita's safety in the event that some "unpleasantness" should occur.

The look his fiery companion gave him assured him that she was nearly as familiar with the breed as he was himself.

"Don't worry about them, baby. I'll take care of you," she said.

"That's funny. I was about to say the same thing myself," Paine replied. He eyed her speculatively as they approached to within several paces of the youths, who looked disinclined to let them peacefully pass. Sullen they were, with alien eyes. There was malice in their faces, hostility in the way they stood.

"Do you mind?" Paine said, stopping just out of range of their hands and feet. He had hoped the white collar and black suit would prevent such a nuisance, but had known it was no guarantee.

"Yeah. We mind," one of them replied belligerently.

"So you've made your point. Now, are you going to get out of the way?" Paine readied himself to move between the three and Torres, regardless of her generous offer to defend him.

The boys were having trouble keeping their nasty in place due to Chita's minimal attire of heels, workout briefs, cropped top, and absolutely nothing else. *Any* comely female bold enough to display her wares in such a fashion would have been a distraction, but *Chita Torres* in that condition could short-circuit the mind.

While Paine was still reviewing his options, she took a step toward the punks and proceeded to fillet them with her tongue. It was a bravura performance, the like of which the rogue had not seen in a long, long time.

In his encyclopedic experience, there were only a few cultures in which ass chewing had been raised until it was on a par with grand opera. The Orientals had a knack for it. The Arabs did, too. But it was the Latins who could do the real star turns. With the French a close second, you couldn't beat an Italian, a Cuban, or a Puerto Rican when it came to inflicting damage with the lips.

Chita sprayed the trio with a torrent of superheated Spanish, much of it too quick for Paine to catch. He was fluent in the language, but not good enough to make the jump to light speed with a native speaker. She used her face and body as artfully and to as deadly an effect as the Gatling gun her voice had become. In swift succession, her expression shifted from outrage to amusement, then to contempt, followed close after by grief, which gave way to frigid menace. Her hands were everywhere, pointing at each of them in turn, waving toward the priest behind her, turning gracefully like birds in flight to touch lightly against her own breast. She swayed. She strutted. She slouched.

Through it all, the trio stood transfixed.

And in the darkness of a doorway across the street, Martina Vlota watched and knew that she must strike while she had the chance, before he slipped away from her again or some others of the legion that hunted him got to John Paine first. She was more heavily armed than ever before, having recently shopped at the local black market herself. On their next and final encounter, nothing would be left to chance. The .45-caliber MAC-10 she had purchased would see to that. She was fully equipped not only to finish him, but anyone who might dare to get in the way, as well.

It wasn't long before Chita Torres had all three of the teenage cutthroats looking uneasy. Regardless of the tattoos and muscle shirts and boots and the rest of the desperado trappings, they still had their fears and lurking superstitions. Torres knew this; knew what they were; and, best of all, knew how to evoke them.

To the best of Paine's understanding, based on the part he could comprehend, it went something like this...

The two of them had just left her mother's deathbed, where Paine had performed the last rites. He was, therefore, cloaked in the dread authority of Holy Mother Church. To interfere with him when he was engaged on such a sacramental mission was to draw down the wrath of God the Father, the Holy Ghost, and the Blessed Virgin Herself. To say nothing of the horde of saints who were always keeping an eye on such things. If the thugs wanted to condemn themselves to hell on earth and purgatory in the Hereafter... that was their decision.

And that was the *good* news.

The bad part was that Chita herself was a priestess of Santoria, the Haitian voodoo cult that was taken very seriously by everyone in the barrio who treasured continued life and health. If they so much as said a cruel word to herself or the priest, she would lay a curse on them that would make them wish they had been born dead. Their genitals would slowly shrink and wither until they eventually fell off. Their bowels would go berserk. They would go blind.

And so on. By the time she had explained what they had to look forward to if they didn't disappear, all three were looking queasy, and Paine was beginning to wonder about her himself.

It was then that the blue-and-white pulled over to the curb beside them to see what all the female screeching was about.

"These scumbags giving you some grief, Father?" The young black patrolman was even larger than Paine himself. The look he gave the youths suggested he might enjoy breaking their bones to let off a little steam.

"Nothing the lady can't handle, Officer, thanks," Paine responded. It was time to move on, he knew, before his luck ran out.

When the cop who was driving leaned over to get a look at his face, Paine looked right back at him. Struggling to look serene and uninvolved under the circumstances was the worst thing he could do.

"You sure everything's okay, Father? We could give you and the lady a ride. This isn't a good place to be on foot at this time of night," the driver said.

The thing that told Paine something was wrong was the way the driver seemed to overlook Chita Torres. That was not the sort of thing that any male who was still breathing was likely to do. But he had eyes only for Paine, and for something that was lying next to him on the seat.

His partner, on the other hand, was so occupied with watching Torres that the driver had to give him a shove to get his attention.

"Come on, Chita," Paine said softly as he took her arm. "It's time for us to move along." As he moved with her down the sidewalk, he called back, "Thanks for the offer, Officer, but I think we'll be all right."

Paine heard one of the cruiser's doors open behind him and almost broke into a run, but decided to bet on grace under pressure instead.

When the driver barked, "You even twitch, Paine, and you are one dead sucker!" the rogue knew he'd lost the bet.

12

Paine knew without turning that the cop had him in his sights. When he heard the other door open, he assumed the number of muzzles pointed at his back had just doubled.

The three delinquents backpedaled off into the night without having to be told. It was a familiar situation. They knew exactly how to respond.

"Take off, bimbo! You don't want any part of this!" the black giant snarled at Torres.

"He's right, Chita. Go home," Paine said. "I'll catch you later." He did not turn to speak to her. He remained very still. If the cops knew his name, they must also know his reputation. Which meant they had their fingers on the triggers. That was too close to eternity for his liking. He would do nothing that might get him closer still.

To her credit, Torres conducted herself with all the street savvy he had come to know that she possessed. She did not protest. She did not try something brave and stupid that was more than likely to get them both killed. Instead, she simply turned and walked away as she was told, her heels making an angry snap with each steady, rapid stride.

"You'll catch her later, all right, *Father*," the

driver said, making his way very cautiously around the car with his service pistol extended in front of him in a solid two-handed grip. "*Much later . . .* as in forty years. Put your hands behind your head and lace the fingers, stud. By the time they let you out of Leavenworth, you'll need spray starch to keep it up. Drop to your knees!"

He maintained a safe distance with the gun trained on Paine while his partner applied the cuffs. They did it well. Professionally. Like men who expected to die for even a slight mistake. Paine knew the South Bronx was the toughest classroom New York City had to offer to the luckless rookies and foul-ups who got assigned to it.

They never moved into one another's line of fire. Never positioned themselves so he could take them both at once. They knew about savage men, men who would go for your throat with their teeth if necessary, men who were willing to get shot a few times before they got to you and removed your eyes.

Paine said nothing and did exactly as he was told. A younger, less-seasoned man might have risked everything to avoid arrest, knowing what that was likely to mean to him. But Paine knew if he made a move, he would certainly have to kill them both. Had they been trying to kill him, he might have done it. They were, however, knowingly risking their lives to take him into custody instead. And he was sure the orders for his apprehension made clear that alive was nice but not mandatory.

So they could have shot him and probably been promoted for it, but, like Paine himself, they were men who lived according to a stark and simple code. Theirs might differ in some particulars from his, but on the whole, they were essentially the same.

You didn't kill anyone who wasn't trying to kill you.

That was one of the commandments that ruled their lives.

The driver held his gun on him while the other cop frisked him. When he found the Desert Eagle and hauled it out into sight, the driver whistled softly and said, "A .44 Mag automatic! No wonder you weren't worried about going for a stroll."

"It was the smallest piece I could find," Paine said somewhat apologetically. He gave the driver a look that said, I'm not a two-bit drug dealer who needs a howitzer to feel secure. The officer, who was the older and more experienced of the pair, nodded and almost smiled.

"So far you're acting like a smart man," the driver said.

"Having guns pointed at me temporarily raises my IQ," Paine said.

"I know what you mean," the driver replied. "The information we have says you are absolutely no one to take chances with. So if you feel a sneeze coming on, you'd better tell us in advance."

"You have my word on it," Paine said.

"I'm not going home in a box for nobody, Paine, so I will blow you up if I have to, but I'd rather not," the younger cop, who was holding the Desert Eagle, said.

"I appreciate that," Paine said.

"If you have another weapon on you, which you probably do, it will help us to relax if you tell us about it. Do you know what I mean?" The black rookie holstered his service pistol, then quickly checked the Desert Eagle to insure that it was loaded and ready to fire before he leveled it on Paine.

"That I do," Paine replied. "You'll find a straight razor in my right sock." They were giving him a chance to defuse the situation somewhat, and he was happy to cooperate.

"Good man," the rookie said. Without lowering the Desert Eagle, he found the razor with his free hand, removed it, and slipped it into the pocket of his trousers.

"Now you're going to get in the back of the cruiser, nice and quiet, right?" the driver asked.

"Right," Paine answered calmly with a nod. "I'm going to stand up now, all right?"

The pair backed away, and Paine rocked his weight back over his heels and rose nimbly to his feet. Both cops noted how easily he managed the difficult maneuver with his hands cuffed behind his back.

"How did you make me? If you don't mind my asking," Paine inquired.

"A couple of Feds dropped by the precinct and passed out about a hundred pictures of you," the driver said. "We've got one on the clipboard on the front seat. They figured you might be hanging around the neighborhood, and they figured right. Let's go."

As they escorted him at a cautious distance to the patrol car, Paine recalled the two well-dressed cannibals from the church. They were apparently as thorough as they were ruthless. Which meant they were top men, as he'd assumed, and worthy opponents. And, unlike his captors, they sought only to cash him out. That made dealing with them far simpler.

All he had to do was kill them first.

Neither the nervous pair in blue, nor the priest who walked between them, took note of the minor altercation that took place a block away as they climbed into the squad car. A swarthy tough much like the ones who'd confronted Paine and Torres forced the driver of a new Buick out of his vehicle at gunpoint, jumped behind the wheel, and drove away, following the cruiser at a discreet distance . . . all the way to its destination.

"What's up? There aren't enough bad guys out there? You have to start busting priests, right?" The heavyset and grizzled desk sergeant looked at Paine and the arresting officers like a trio of Jehovah's Witnesses with copies of *The Watchtower* in hand.

"I offered to grant them absolution if they'd let me go," Paine said, "but they weren't buying it. Must have pretty clean slates, I guess."

"What the hell's going on here?" the sergeant growled.

"This is the government hit man those two Feds are looking for," the driver said. "He's wanted for murder and treason and kidnapping, and damn near anything else you can think of."

"*You* are John Paine?" the sergeant asked. The growl dropped suddenly to a tone that was far more subdued.

"The same. Makes you want to go for your gun, doesn't it?" Paine surveyed the stained and stinking bull pen in which the sergeant's desk was centered. The place had "end of the road" written all over it. There were hookers and thieves and junkies scattered around the room in various stages of processing.

"Take him up to the holding cell for the time being. Are we supposed to book him or what?" The sergeant looked dubious about the presence of such a big-league criminal in a sandlot station house like his own.

"I think we're just supposed to hold him until the Feds get here, Sergeant," the driver said.

So they can cart me off to someplace nice and

private where there won't be any witnesses to what logically comes next, Paine thought.

"All right! So do it," the sergeant grumbled. "This whole business reeks. The Feds should clean up their own messes without getting us involved. We got plenty of messes of our own."

"I'll leave if it would make you feel better," Paine volunteered.

"And how does this make us look! Marching a guy around in cuffs who's dressed up like a priest! For Chrissakes, people will think we got no respect." The sergeant shook his head disgustedly and dropped his face into one meaty hand.

"I tried to explain that to them myself, but they weren't having any," Paine said.

"Come on, Paine," the rookie said, taking him by the arm and guiding him toward the stairs at the end of the room.

"Why didn't they have any big, bad dudes like you when *I* was goin' to church?" The leggy red-headed streetwalker leered drunkenly at Paine as the partners escorted him past.

"Back off, Irene," the driver said, waving her out of the way with one slicing hand.

"You pigs will go to hell for this! You can't treat a man of God that way!" It was a faceless voice bellowing from behind their backs.

"You worried?" Paine asked, glancing at the driver.

"Not much. Hell would be an improvement after the South Bronx," he said.

They walked Paine up the stairs, and as they did . . .

Martina Vlota pulled the stolen Buick into the alley beside the station. When she stepped out, she left the motor running. What she was about to do would not . . . *could not* take very long. She had Paine where she wanted him now. In a box. The NYPD was making it easy for her. She was pleased to avail herself of their unwitting assistance. The number of those who would have to die so that she could repay him for hurling her into the sea that night so long before was of no more than academic interest to her. All that truly mattered was that *he* should know that *she* would be the one to take his life in the end, thus proving once and for all time which of them was the better. And then to make good her escape.

Vlota unbuttoned the loose shirt that concealed the chunky black, short-barreled MAC-10 machine pistol and the extra magazines she carried with her. One last time she yanked the slide back to be sure a round was chambered. Then she strolled confidently toward the front door. She knew she was better-armed and better-trained than any of those who stood between her and the rogue.

She knew, too, that she had the upper hand because, for her, killing was a pleasure. The young patrolman she had abducted in order to flee when her last attempt at Paine was foiled had not known that. Thus, he had assumed she would spare his life if he did as he was told. Even when she'd made him kneel before her in a safe and desolate place, he had clung to that fond hope.

But at the last instant he had known. Vlota was glad for that. When she touched the Heckler and Koch automatic to his lips, he had recognized the distant look in her eyes. Vlota had shot him at that instant before he could do something that might spoil that delicate moment. There were certain acts that demanded precision to achieve their highest form, and executions were foremost among them.

* * *

"Looks like you get the Presidential Suite all to yourself, Paine," the rookie said as he unlocked the handcuffs before Paine entered the holding cell. It was not so much a cell as it was a simple cage in one corner of the detectives' squad room on the building's second floor.

"You're all heart," Paine said. He stood back away from the bars as the driver turned the key to lock the door. Then Paine watched as the patrolman carried the key on its ring over to the far wall, where he hung it on a nail that projected from it at eye level.

As Paine was wondering if it might not be a good time to put in a request for his last meal, Martina Vlota mounted the steps and crossed the threshold below, determined that he would not have time for it.

"Gun!" was the last word the desk sergeant would ever roar. He spotted Vlota as she entered, and being unarmed, he was forced to drop behind the desk for cover and pray that reinforcements were on the way. They *were*, but the barking burst of .45 slugs she put through the desk insured they would be of no benefit to him when they arrived.

Upstairs, the partners who had apprehended Paine heard it all and knew an invasion of some kind was under way. They were sprinting toward the stairs even as they went for their holstered pistols, leaving Paine alone in the room behind them in the cage.

As more gunfire of various calibers erupted on the floor below, Paine knew in his gut that his appointed hour had finally arrived. Someone who wanted him had opted for the direct approach. No more games. No more subterfuge. They had him staked out and defenseless, and it was too good an opportunity to let slide.

Vlota roamed the bull pen and the adjacent

rooms, killing the boys and girls in blue wherever she found them. She held the MAC in the pre-scribed combat position, gripping it hard with both hands, keeping her elbows braced tight against her sides. She stayed close to the walls, pivoting her lithe body toward each new frantic target as it popped up. She was no novice to such close-quarters combat, but her opponents were, and she knew that.

They had no programmed reactions to what was happening. Vlota had known the element of shock would give her another great advantage, and she used it to the full. The screams of the wounded mingled with the gun smoke and the staccato thunder of the MAC to intensify the panic that smashed through the building like a lethal tidal wave.

When the partners hurtled down the stairs with their guns in their hands, they encountered the mad stampede among the riffraff with whom the room was filled. Whores and hypes and miscel-laneous felons of all descriptions were scrambling in any direction that seemed to hold some promise of survival.

Into that boiling, colorful mosaic, Martina Vlota blended, becoming no more than another element in the swirling scenery, but every badge and every uniform stood out loud and clear.

The black rookie and the driver crouched side by side at the foot of the stairs, searching, knowing they must hold their fire lest some innocents should die in a hail of indiscriminate cross fire.

Vlota saw them where she knelt to swiftly eject a spent magazine and ram a fresh one into the MAC. She was in a corridor that ran between a series of offices and interrogation rooms, none of which had contained the object of her blind hate. Unlike the two partners, Vlota was happy to waste any civilian who got in the way.

"There he is!" The rookie finally saw her and indicated her position to the veteran next to him with the muzzle of his .38 Smith. He opened fire, and seconds later, the driver squeezed the nine-millimeter Colt automatic in his hands. The crack of the service revolver was submerged beneath the roar of the more powerful weapon next to it. Both spit tongues of flame as the barrels bucked and dropped repeatedly.

Vlota heard the first round whistle inches above her head before it ripped into the wall behind her, glancing away to bury itself in the hallway's other wall. She dropped and rolled, and the fusillade followed her down. There was fifty feet between them. A difficult shot for a handgun. Especially when the target was small and moving fast. Still, Vlota could hear the spinning lead heating the air around her; could see the bites the bullets were tearing from the floor.

She triggered the MAC, shooting low, oblivious to the men and women desperately clinging to the bull pen floor over which she fired. A head was raised at that moment, and was magically disassembled and showered over the cowering mob. Her first salvo savaged the stairs between the two, filling the air around them with wood slivers and a confetti of ancient linoleum. The rookie was speed-loading the Smith when she fired again, and four slugs took him square in the center from the belly to the throat. As big as he was, he was slammed back onto the risers, where he lay quivering and pumping out a crimson flood. Across from him, the driver held his stance and continued to fire. He put a nine-millimeter slug in the floor in front of Vlota's face, and it should have ricocheted. Should have careened up to finish her, its momentum only slightly diminished. But it drove into the wood instead, simply spraying her with exploding particles of debris. When Vlota fired again, emptying the magazine, the storm of slugs seized and lifted and spun him, throwing him onto his face on the stairs. The two cops lay there shoulder to shoulder, pressed as close in death as they had ever been in life.

Vlota tensed, ready for another blue silhouette to appear. When none did, and a sudden jarring silence filled the room, she rose and dashed to the stairs. Three at a time, she took them, easily hurdling the bodies of the men that blocked her way.

John Paine was standing in the cage waiting for her when she reached the second floor.

When she saw him, Vlota snorted triumphantly.

"Bastard! Now you are mine!" She jogged over to the cell, smiling, her dark eyes alight, and leveled the MAC-10 on his chest.

Unfortunately, Paine was able to find no flaws in that statement. "Looks like you got it right, for once," he said emotionlessly.

"I only regret I haven't the time to make it last like what you did to me," she snarled. Her sexless face was a portrait of seething malice.

"You tried to kill me, Vlota, and you blew it. That's what got you the long swim in the Adriatic. Why don't you admit it?" Paine said. He saw little point in talking it over, knowing he wasn't likely to change her mind, but whatever the shortcomings of conversation with her, it beat hell out of getting shot.

"I suppose you would have made it quick for me if I'd only given you the chance!" she sneered.

"That's right," Paine answered. "You're the one with a real taste for it, not me. That's why you closed in to finish me, and when you did, gave me my chance. If you'd done it like a professional, I would have been the one who went over the side instead of you." For what little good it did, he enjoyed the opportunity to point out the way it really was. Even coming from a lunatic like Vlota, he found it offensive to be branded a sadist. Killing had always been a trade for him, not a form of recreation. Among more gentle folk, that might seem a frivolous distinction, but among his kind, it made all the difference in the world.

"You are an arrogant boor to the very end, aren't you?" she hissed, stepping closer to the bars, close enough to insert the short barrel of the MAC between them.

"And you are a vicious, bloodthirsty dyke... which puts me out in the lead, in my humble opinion." Paine kept his eyes riveted to her face when he detected the stealthy motion behind her in his peripheral vision.

Paine almost smiled when he realized that Martina Vlota's talent for turning victory into defeat was running terminally true to form.

13

"Do you have anything else to say before I start at your knees? Perhaps if you apologize, I might start with your ugly head instead." Vlota's face was rapidly losing its venom. Paine found it a strange and unsettling phenomenon to closely observe. It was as if a drain plug had been pulled in the basement of her brain, and all feeling was swiftly siphoning out of her. It was rendered all the more disturbing because he knew what it meant. She was slipping into that cold, pseudosexual frame of mind that arose in her when an execution was imminent.

Paine had to call up all his self-control to keep from glancing at whoever it was who was getting into position behind her. He dare not give the person away with the slightest telltale sign. Vlota was cobra-fast. He could do nothing that would provide her with a warning. Nonetheless, he moved as casually as he could away from what looked like the line of fire. Paine did his best to act like a man whose nerve was fading on him. Fading enough, at least, to push him steadily backward and to his right until his broad shoulders were wedged into the corner of the cage.

"What would really turn you on would be hav-

ing me strapped to a rack in a dungeon somewhere, right? They still have that sort of scene
back where you come from, don't they? Thumbscrews, branding irons, whips and chains. The
whole Boris Karloff routine," Paine said. He was
running out of clever things to say that might
keep her trigger finger relaxed for a few more
seconds. If the person behind her was coming to
his rescue, *now* would be as good a time as any.

"You read my mind," Vlota said with an air of
ominous detachment. "But I'm afraid this will
have to do."

"Vlota." Her name was spoken softly by the man
who had stolen in with all the sure silence of a
stalking leopard to join them.

Paine was on his way to the floor a heartbeat
before Vlota began to turn. He would never know
why she didn't shoot him then, when it would have
been so easy. It was probably the surprise, he assumed; the unexpected use of her name. Or, perhaps, it was simply her last major mistake.

Sensing that she was out of time, Vlota opened
fire before she was fully turned. It was a desperate
act, and one that failed to save her.

Mikhail Nikita Godunov did not speak until he
had taken cover behind a desk twenty feet away,
with Martina Vlota securely in his sights. He
would not have spoken at all had anyone but John
Paine been her intended victim. For all her fail-
ings, Vlota was to be taken most seriously if your
objective was to kill her, and his was. But Godunov had both respect and affection for the rogue,
based on mutual past experience. Thus, it was
necessary to get the woman to turn before he took
her.

With that little nightmare in her hands, if her
finger locked over the trigger when she was hit,
she might very well fire all thirty rounds as she

went down. That made removing her without removing John Paine at the same time an extremely touchy trick, to Godunov's way of thinking.

Having a rather intellectual turn of mind, the Russian saw the whole thing as much like a difficult chess maneuver. Being more devoutly committed to his own ongoing survival than to that of Paine, he waited not a millisecond longer than he had to, with the massive stainless steel match-grade Sokolovsky .45 automatic held firmly in his manicured right hand, before he opened fire.

The field operative for Soviet military intelligence was no fool. He was also the GRU's most decorated and senior agent. So he was highly disinclined toward anything fancy. As the MAC-10 raged, spewing slugs through the doorway and into the stairwell to his right, Godunov shot Martina Vlota six times as fast as he could squeeze the trigger; placed all six rounds in the center of her chest, in a fist-sized grouping, between her firm, diminutive breasts.

Her body slammed back against the cage and was held there by each ensuing slug. The machine pistol flew, as if clubbed, from her grasp. She hung there for moments after Godunov fired the sixth and final time. The chilly, murderous expression had been erased completely from her face. In its stead there was that look that Godunov had seen so many times before. She gaped, stunned and astonished that Death had finally overtaken her, as if she never expected it to happen. Not to her. Not really.

Then the portrait went slack and faded, the eyes emptied; her slender body collapsed to the floor; and the being that was Martina Vlota went somewhere else to be with others like herself.

"You couldn't have waited a little longer, could you?" Paine rifled the remark at Godunov as he rose to his feet inside the cell, finding, to his considerable disgust, that he had Vlota's blood spattered on his clerical garb.

The dapper GRU man wore a light summer-weight suit of snowy linen, with stylish straw hat and Gucci loafers to match. Paine thought he looked as sorely out of place as a vintage Ferrari in the midst of a landfill.

Having spotted the key on the wall, Godunov detoured over to pluck it from the nail on his way to his friend's cell.

"You needn't have worried, John," Godunov said, stepping carefully around Vlota's corpse to get to the lock. "I have yet to meet the Albanian who would not pause to gloat at great length in such a situation, and she was worse than the average. So much worse, in fact, that they decided she had become an embarrassment even by their standards." He opened the door for Paine and began to move off toward the stairs. "Watch your step, John."

"So they gave her to the GRU?" He paused for a moment outside the cell to stare down at the bloody remains of the woman who had pursued him so far and for so long, gleefully killing so many along the way.

"That's right," Godunov replied. "Let's move along, shall we? Someone might mistake us for Albanians if we gloat." He gave Paine one of his odd, uneven smiles with arching brows. He was as aristocratic about the face as ever, nonetheless, with his mane of sweeping gray and the equally gray, immaculate mustache and beard. "This place is also going to get very crowded, very soon, I think."

"I'm right behind you," Paine said.

They made their way quickly down the stairs and through the killing ground the first floor had become. Their passage was barely noted by those who had survived unscathed. The atmosphere of the place was dense with the shock that followed close on any such disaster.

"She left a car running in the alley," Godunov said as they sped through the doors, down the steps, and onto the walk in front. "It is no doubt stolen, but it will do to get us out of the area."

"Looks like I owe you one," Paine said from the passenger side of the front seat once they were several blocks away.

"Who keeps score, John?" Godunov replied.

"I do. This puts you one ahead," Paine said. He winced from a flare of pain in his side. He'd landed on the cracked ribs when he hit the deck in the cage.

"Whatever you say. Far be it from me to argue with a priest," Godunov replied. He glanced at Paine's costume with a look that was wryly amused. "I'd say everything's worked out rather nicely, wouldn't you? Except for the slaughter, of course. That's quite tragic. It's a damn shame it had to happen, but as it turned out, it was them or you. If I were more *civic-minded*, we wouldn't be having this conversation, I don't suppose." When he cut his eyes once again toward Paine, they shone with a dark and sardonic light.

"Why don't you just lay it out for me and spare us both a lot of stupid questions?" Paine said.

"Very well, old man. An excellent idea." When he spoke English, Godunov came across like British upper crust due to his education at Oxford and Cambridge. When he spoke his native tongue, however, it was with the unmistakable stamp of the Leningrad proletariat from which he'd sprung. He was one of the most intriguing sanction specialists John Paine had ever encountered. Paine was secretly glad his past efforts to terminate Godunov had been unsuccessful. Primarily because if they had been, there would have been no one there to interfere with Vlota's plans for him minutes before. But beyond that, the Russian's death would have rendered the world a significantly less interesting place.

"I didn't get the go-ahead on her termination until yesterday," Godunov continued. "Her countrymen could have done it themselves, of course, but being the hopeless toadies that they are, they saw it as a fine chance to score some points with the GRU, whom they live in constant fear of offending."

"And well they should," Paine interjected. The brutal effectiveness of Soviet military intelligence was sufficient to daunt even the world's leading intelligence organizations. Small wonder it should make the blood of the Albanian spy masters run cold.

"It seems they concluded that her recreational approach to killing was going to draw fire on them before long. They knew we had a score to settle with her. So giving her to us impressed them as a brilliant solution to the problem she had become. I must admit I find it somewhat inspired myself. It's far more cunning than I ever would have expected from the Albanians." They had crossed over the East River into Harlem by way of the Third Avenue Bridge from the Bronx. Godunov was looking for a likely dismal block on which to dump the car before they went in search of a taxi on one of the major thoroughfares. As the Russian had known, in that infamous sector of Manhattan, there was no shortage of desolate streets to choose from.

"Though she was pursuing a personal matter, Vlota was still on the leash, so she checked in with her control regularly," Godunov continued.

"So they were able to put me on to her immediately. I assumed that finding her would also mean finding you, given what you had already told me about her pursuit. I did not expect, however, to arrive on the scene at such a critical moment." He pulled the Buick to the curb in front of an especially disreputable-looking bar, turned to Paine, and said, "I believe this will do nicely for a disposal site, don't you?"

"I couldn't have chosen one better myself, Nikki," Paine replied. "With the keys in it, I'd say it should be stolen and stripped in a couple of hours at the outside."

The two assassins were an unlikely-looking pair as they strolled and chatted their way through the sultry midnight darkness of the nation's best-known ghetto. Despite their dandy and sedate attire, however, none of the local predators was too tempted to test them. It could have been no more than the fearless ease with which both moved. Or it might have been the rogue's black bulk. Or something decidedly reptilian in the Russian's continuously sweeping eyes. Whatever it was, they were closely scrutinized a number of times, but always left alone.

"So Vlota was watching me when I got busted, and you were watching her," Paine speculated.

"Precisely," Godunov replied. "And I must say your taste in women, if *taste* is the word, has not changed appreciably since we first met."

"Your envy is showing, Nikki. You wouldn't chase all those anemic artsy types if you thought you could keep up with a woman like Chita Torres long enough to do her any good," Paine said. Their radically different tastes in women was another subject on which they differed at one another's good-natured expense whenever their paths crossed.

"Those *anemic artsy types*, as you so generously call them, are at least bright enough to hold up their end of the conversation between couplings," Godunov rejoined.

"That in-between part must cover a lot of territory for a man like you, right?" Paine asked mock-seriously. "That's why you need a real Ivy League talker on the other side of the bed. Personally, I keep my women too busy catching their breath to get in more than an occasional obscene word or two."

"And that is definitely what that item you were with appeared capable of," Godunov parried. "Be that as it may, I realized when they took you into custody that there was probably no peaceful way to extract you from it before your employer dispatched someone dependable to...how is it the mobsters put it in the movies...*take you for a ride?*"

"That's the way they put it, all right," Paine responded. "So you figured Vlota would probably see that as her chance; would blow away my jailers to get to me; and if you timed it right, you could whack her before she whacked me. Then the two of us could walk away with damn near everyone doing fine except Vlota and New York's finest."

"That's about it," Godunov agreed. "If you hadn't been thrown into the equation, I'd have certainly tried to take her before the tally of her victims became any greater than it was. But the fact was, I had no obligation to defend the police. That was *their* responsibility. If they'd managed to kill her, I don't know what I could have done on your behalf, if anything. However, since she was the victor, I simply took advantage of their defeat like the inveterate opportunist that I am." Godunov looked at Paine and shrugged.

"Unfortunately for the NYPD, they were badly

outclassed. Fortunately for me, so was she. Thanks, Nikki." Paine extended his hand. Godunov nodded silently and gave it a quick, hard squeeze.

"In my place, you would have done as much," Godunov said dismissively. "So what do you do now? You realize, of course, that all of that bloodshed back there will be credited to you, or as much of it as your enemies can arrange."

"Why should this time be different? I think it's time for another visit to D.C. There's a man there I need to talk to. Maybe he can shed some light on the situation," Paine said. They had reached a through street. Taxis were passing regularly, headed downtown. The two men took turns hailing them in the time-honored New York manner, wondering when one of them would be kind enough to stop.

"You mean to say you actually know someone in the game who isn't trying to kill you?" Godunov asked skeptically.

"I didn't say that. He's the man who recruited me. I can't say for sure which side he's on at the moment," Paine said.

"As long as you don't trust him, John, we'll probably meet again." Godunov looked hard into his friend's eyes.

"Don't worry. You just saved my life, and I don't trust *you*."

"Very good. But just in case your paranoia slips, how about breakfast on me? For old times' sake, yes?" Godunov stepped out into the street with Paine as a taxi suddenly veered over to them.

"If you're buying, we can eat for any damn reason you please, Nikki," the rogue replied.

14

"Hello?" Walter Hapgood said. He was at home in suburban Maryland, seated at the desk in his study.

"Hello, Walter. I think it's time for our talk," the familiar voice said.

"It's good to hear from you, John. Are you all right?" Hapgood punched the "Record" button on the tape machine next to the phone.

"All things considered, Walter, I'm fine; and you?" Paine replied. He listened closely for any tinge of tension or guilt in his recruiter's voice, any indication that he was something other than the old, reliable friend that he appeared to be, but all he heard was warm concern. Which didn't necessarily mean that this was the emotion he was experiencing as he spoke. Hapgood was an even older hand than Paine himself.

"As you say, John, all things considered, I can't complain. The wife and our two youngest are at the summer place in the Hamptons, spending my money faster than I can make it. That's the closest thing I have to a gripe. Are you in the vicinity again?" Hapgood asked.

"Yes, I am," Paine replied. "At the moment I'm

at a pay phone across the street from the Bureau's headquarters."

Hapgood smiled grimly at the phone. That was certainly the John Paine he knew. At last check, he was fourth on the FBI's Most Wanted list, and he felt free to make himself comfortable in their backyard. "You thinking about dropping in to see if they could use a helping hand?"

"The thought had occurred to me. I know they must be feeling pretty frustrated these days. Speaking of frustration, how are things at the office?" Paine inquired.

"Brock has been making human sacrifices ever since that stunt you pulled at his daughter's wedding reception. Really, John, you're going to push your luck too far one of these days." Hapgood let an irritation show in his voice that had as much to do with his killers' failure as with the reign of terror the Director had instituted at Langley after his humiliation at the hands of the rogue.

"I hope the humor of the thing wasn't lost on all my colleagues," Paine said.

"Don't worry. It wasn't. Among those who still believe in your loyalty, and there are more of us than you might think, there are some who found it amusing to the point of nearly losing their heads over it," Hapgood said.

"But you are not among them," Paine speculated.

"A man in my position does well to approach most things very seriously of late," Hapgood intoned. "I'm sure you know whereof I speak." It was Hapgood's way of politely reminding Paine that his neck was on the block for having recruited the now notorious "traitor and psychopath." The slightest indiscretion, like an inappropriate laugh, could bring the headsman's ax whistling down.

"Yes. Of course. Perhaps the two of us together can find a solution to this. I've come up with a plan for our meeting that should keep us securely in the black," Paine said. *In the black* was shorthand in the game for keeping free of prying ears and eyes.

"I thought you might," Hapgood replied. It was no less than he expected from a man of Paine's experience and innate caution. Regardless of any trust Paine might still feel toward him, the rogue would approach their meeting like a patrol behind enemy lines during time of war.

"Do you have a piece of paper handy?" Paine asked.

"Yes. Right here. Go ahead," Hapgood responded.

It took five minutes for Paine to give him all the details for a nocturnal rendezvous two days hence in a suitably remote location.

"Now, read that back to me," Paine requested. He wanted to be sure that his recruiter was taking the offered bait with all of his teeth.

Hapgood repeated the instructions slowly, detail by elaborate detail.

"Good, Walter. I'm looking forward to seeing you," Paine said.

"No less than I, John. Until then, watch your step," Hapgood advised, like the protective uncle he once had been.

"Always, Walter. You do that, too, won't you?"

As soon as they rang off, Hapgood put a call through to New York City, to the answering service he was using to stay in touch with Strado and Thomas. The message was simple: Take the next plane back/Contact immediately.

He was calling in the wolves for what he hoped would be the last act in the play. Hapgood felt a twinge of guilt at the betrayal. John Paine had never done him anything but good. But there were times when a man had to do harsh things to survive. This was, sadly but certainly, one of those times. And even with the element of betrayal working to his advantage, it was not going to be without considerable risk. He had not worked in the field for far too long. He'd lost his feel for it. A *feel* that John Paine possessed to a greater degree than any other agent Hapgood had ever known.

He found it hateful and frightening to have to use himself as the "cheese" when the predator to be seduced into the trap was so huge and so given to reflexive, homicidal violence. Hapgood was also only too familiar with the chapter in Paine's personal book of ethics that dealt with betrayal by old friends. He didn't care to recall the paragraph that covered the penalty for that ultimate crime. It was disturbing enough to know that if the ambush should fail, it would be Hapgood himself standing between the jagged teeth when the jaws of the trap slammed shut.

However, now that Paine had shaken his pursuers in New York City, Hapgood could see no other worthy option available to him. He contented himself with the belief that "Plan 'B' " was and always had been surer and more likely to succeed than its predecessor. Paine's knack for saving his own neck was no less than preternatural. If there was the slightest flaw in a plot against him, the man would discover and make use of it.

Sullivan Stith, Hapgood now realized, had been that flaw. Paine had chewed up and spit out that particular brute in an almost casual manner. Appropriately enough, Stith's final contribution to the mission had been to ruin it with his untimely death.

It was only hours before that Hapgood had learned of the massacre at the precinct station in the South Bronx. He was still lacking in sufficient information to make sense of it. All that seemed clear were the gore-laden basic elements of the situation. Paine had been miraculously taken into custody without a shot being fired; he'd been locked up securely to await the arrival of Strado and Thomas, after which his earthly hours would have been numbered in the single digits; a firefight had taken place in which a total of sixteen police officers and civilians had lost their lives; and when the smoke cleared and the screaming stopped, John Paine had made good his escape.

The man was unnaturally difficult to destroy.

God help those who try for him and fail, Hapgood murmured prayerfully in his mind.

He knew that applied to him, personally, in the very near future. He vowed to make extremely clear to his eager young killers that if they muffed their second chance at Paine, after Hapgood risked his hide to set it up, the next termination order he handed out might have two names on it that they would find most familiar. They had wanted their shot at the "big leagues," and they had gotten it.

Now they must realize what striking out meant in the "majors."

Paine was able to "exchange" the 450SL Mercedes he had "borrowed" at Dulles International for a sporty new Mazda Miata a few minutes after his call to Hapgood was completed. In his experience, if a stolen car was never used for longer than six hours, the chance of a bulletin being broadcast with its description was next to nil. For the time being, he intended to stick with vehicles that stood a good chance of outrunning or outmaneuvering a squadron of police cruisers. After his recent experience in the South Bronx, he no longer considered it safe to assume every cop in the country couldn't recognize him on sight.

He took the first ramp he encountered that would put him on the freeway going in the direction of Walter Hapgood's suburban home. The first motel that looked sufficiently large and anonymous along the way would suffice for the rest he badly needed. Then his close surveillance of his recruiter would begin.

Paine had never intended to carry through with the clandestine meeting, the details of which he had calculated with such care for Hapgood's benefit. That was no more than a ruse, a safeguard against the possibility that the man was not as trustworthy as he seemed. Paine sincerely hoped that that was not the case. In that event, no harm would have been done to anything but Hapgood's feelings by the deception.

If his recruiter *had* turned on him, however, then the absence of harm would be to Paine himself. It was a classic ploy the rogue had employed regularly throughout the years when there was reason to fear an ambush at the appointed place and time. While the other party concentrated on perfecting the snare into which Paine was scheduled to stroll, Paine would be stalking him and preparing to make their meeting a less formal and more impromptu sort of affair.

Paine saw it as another variation on the time-tested theme that survival and unpredictability usually traveled hand in hand. The more the world at large knew about who you were, and how you functioned, and where you could be found, the less your chances that you would forever postpone the arrival of the Great and Final Surprize.

Just ask the ghost of Martina Vlota. She had

known that her control could be trusted with her whereabouts. That control was probably someone she had worked with closely and trusted for years. Long enough to forget that the person would kill her, or help someone else to do the job, if the day ever came when that seemed *necessary*.

Necessity, Paine knew, was a very large issue in his chosen trade. It determined who was willing to do what to whom and when. Only if you were absolutely sure of what the other man's perceived necessity might be could you reliably predict how he would act.

It wasn't enough to base your decision on a preponderance of the available evidence. That would get you close, but it wasn't one of those games, like horseshoes and hand grenades, where close was good enough. No. You had to be dead certain unless you were willing to be dead dead.

And John Paine was not dead certain about Hapgood.

So he was waiting in a freshly stolen car the next afternoon when Hapgood's Lincoln Town Car cruised away from Langley, headed in the direction of D.C. He gave Hapgood an ample lead before he pulled onto the road behind him, knowing that such a rolling billboard of conspicuous consumption could be followed easily from a great distance, up to and including outer space.

Paine was prepared to follow his recruiter home, if that was where the man went, confident that wherever he intercepted him, his sudden appearance would be equally unexpected. However, when the Lincoln took an exit into one of the capital's less savory districts, Paine concluded that Hapgood had something more adventurous than a TV dinner and the evening news in mind.

"Adventurous" was replaced by "licentious"

when the Town Car pulled into the discreetly concealed parking lot behind a cheap-looking single-story concrete block structure with "Rhonda's Retreat" inscribed in tubular neon across the front. Paine knew there were a score of other, nearly identical "retreats" in that immediate area. All advertised an array of equally identical, and equally irrelevant, services to their exclusively male clientele.

Paine couldn't recall offhand if he had ever encountered such a place that simply and straightforwardly called itself a "Massage Parlor." That was what everyone, including their employees, called them, but their proprietors seemed unwilling to be that blunt about the business they were conducting. Paine assumed such commercial coyness was based upon the same reasoning that kept certain other capitalists from using "Whorehouse" in the title of *their* establishments.

It remained a mystery to him, however, since no one, from crusading evangelists to cops to the average half-bright civilian, was fooled by the smoke screens they all used. That it might in some way be connected with the nation's apparently inescapable Puritan heritage, Paine was willing to grudgingly acknowledge. However, since history had never been one of his strong suits, he had to leave a definitive answer to whatever chroniclers of play-for-pay in the U.S. of A. there might be.

Paine watched from a distance as Hapgood locked the Lincoln and paused to see if the coast was clear with the painfully casual air of a neophyte bank robber. Evidently his remark about the family being out of town had been the truth. The cat was away, and the mouse was scurrying to a pleasure palace while the time was ripe.

Well, to err was human. It was the way of all

flesh. And so on. The rogue had, however, expected slightly more in the way of good taste from his venerable recruiter. Rhonda's neighborhood was one of those where "down and dirty" ruled supreme. It was, in fact, the sort of sleazy locale where Paine felt right at home.

Paine decided the setting was close to ideal for a secret meeting. From *his* standpoint, at least. It was unlikely that Walter Hapgood would relish being caught with his pants down. It took someone more like Chita Torres to handle that sort of thing with real aplomb. But all was supposedly fair in love and war, and the rogue had been at war since birth.

When Paine entered the reception area of Rhonda's Retreat in his recently cleaned and pressed black suit, crisp black shirt, and sparkling white collar, there was one young woman standing behind the counter. On a couch across from her, two more damsels sat trading gossip, smoking, and obviously killing time. All three were dressed for the intense summer heat despite the fact that the air-conditioning kept it outside, where it belonged.

The trio stared at him for a while, then at one another, then back at him again, as if to reassure themselves that he wasn't a mirage. One of the pair on the couch suddenly broke into a giggle. She was a slender, leggy, green-eyed blonde with a ponytail that extended below her narrow waist. Her hand flew up in the unsuccessful effort to stifle the giggle an instant before she caught an elbow from her companion. The girl beside her, a deeply tanned redhead with amber eyes who was built along more muscular, athletic lines, might have been a Catholic. She sat up straight from the sensual slouch she'd been in and tried to look as prim as she could under the circumstances.

The one behind the counter, who seemed to be the manager, was a brunette with a boyishly close haircut that didn't make her look like a boy. As appealing as she was, her look and manner were of the regular, girl-next-door variety, which made her seem somewhat out of place in a massage parlor, as if she might have gotten the job by mistake, and had yet to discover what was going on in the warren of dimly lighted cubicles in back.

She appeared to be a few years older than the other two, and from the businesslike expression with which she regarded him, Paine expected her to ask if he would be using Visa or Mastercard. What she said instead was, "One of us is in the wrong place, Father, and I don't think it's me."

"What's the problem, my child? Your sign says you have a whirlpool and steam room available. This is a health club, isn't it?" Paine couldn't resist having a little fun with them, given the nature of his disguise.

"Well . . . sort of." The brunette started chewing her lower lip as she wrestled with the prospect of admitting a priest into the midst of all the intense "relaxation" that was taking place in pairs behind the false wall that separated them from the rest of the establishment.

"I don't suppose it matters anyway," Paine continued, knowing it was time to proceed with his meeting before Hapgood became too involved with his "therapy" to think straight about anything else. "I'm not here to avail myself of the many expert talents I'm sure you all possess."

The manager relaxed visibly at that, as did the redhead on the couch. However, the blonde seated next to her seemed, if anything, a trifle disappointed.

"I happened to notice an old friend of mine entering as I was driving by," Paine explained. "A hefty, gray-haired gentleman in a three-piece suit. It's most important that I speak with him for a few minutes. Do you think that could be arranged?"

The brunette appeared to find that idea about as appealing as taking the priest's money and handing him a towel. The sort of encounters that took place in Rhonda's Retreat were not the kind that the customers cared to have interrupted by surprize visits from old acquaintances. Of any description. Least of all, understandably, if the old acquaintance happened to be a priest. The embarrassment potential of the situation was second only to a vice squad raid.

"I'm afraid you'll have to wait for him out here, Father. We guarantee our customers the complete privacy they need to relax," the brunette said flatly with a slight, but final, shake of her head. He had *his* Bible, and she had *hers*. And in *hers*, what he was proposing was a mortal sin.

"I understand completely," Paine said, "but you have my assurance that he will be very forgiving about the interruption. The matter I have to discuss with him is every bit as important to him as it is to me, and he knows that."

"Sorry," she said with another shake of her head, "no can do. I'd get fired in a New York minute if the boss found out I let you do that."

When Paine removed a thick wad of one-hundred-dollar bills from his trouser pocket, the looks on the faces of all three lovelies revealed that the conversation had just entered a whole new phase.

"I realize this is a headache for you. Would a thousand dollars... apiece... ease the pain?" He glanced from the manager to the two girls on the couch as he swiftly peeled one bill after another off the roll. Paine knew it was one of those places where "money" was spoken with greater fluency than it was in most. No one had been known to work in a massage parlor for the status.

"I don't know..." the brunette replied hesitantly. She was making a valiant attempt to hold on to her professional resolve, but it looked like her grip was fading fast.

"Maaaanndyyyy!" the blonde hissed from the couch with a look that could easily have butchered a steer. "That's what I make in a *month*! If you don't take him back, I *will*! It's not like he's never seen a hard-on before!" She stopped abruptly after she said it, her eyes darting up to Paine as if she had momentarily forgotten he was there. When she saw the amused look on his face, she realized he was not nearly as naive as he had seemed. Which inspired her to add, "Right, Father?" with a playful grin.

"More than once, believe it or not. I was a man of the world before I donned the cloth," Paine replied. He gave her a far-from-celibate look when he handed her the grand.

"I'll bet you were," the blonde said huskily. "If you have a little time to spare after your talk, just let me know, okay? A thousand dollars will buy you one incredible massage." Her emerald eyes promised him a kaleidoscope of delights he would never find in church.

"It would be heavenly, I'm sure," Paine responded from the heart. "I'll keep your offer in mind."

"You do that, Father," the blonde said.

Paine proceeded to hand a thousand to the redhead and then to the manager, as agreed. Once she had the money in hand, the all-American brunette braced herself, looked him in the eye, and said, "If you'll just walk this way." Then she stepped from behind the counter, her high heels rapping on the shiny tile floor, and strutted over to the curtain that separated the business from the entertainment at Rhonda's Retreat.

"I look funny enough without doing that," he muttered as he studied her high, trim derriere and the way it rhythmically flexed.

He followed her down a long, carpeted corridor with closed doors on either side until she stopped at the fourth one on the left and softly knocked. Paine found himself eavesdropping unconsciously on any lusty sounds that might escape from any of the cubicles they had passed. It was either a better-constructed place than it looked or he had arrived during an intermission. The silence was not so much as rippled by a sigh.

Before the brunette could knock again, before the door could open, Paine gently pushed the young woman aside, taking her place in front of it. Moments later, the door was eased open quietly by a teenager with a collar-length helmet of hair like crude oil and a face to make the angels weep. As soon as she saw the man who hulked on the other side, her flawless brow furrowed into a deep scowl.

"Yes? What do you want?" she whispered. Her voice was dusky and deep, and it served to enhance her already considerable gifts. Those gifts were prominently on display at the time. She wore only underpants of the brightest pink.

Paine put a finger to his lips, then crooked it to beckon her into the hall. Before she could object, he grasped her wrist and tugged her over the threshhold. She made no effort to conceal two of the firmest, fullest, palest orbs Paine had seen in many a moon.

"Nice outfit," he said softly as he passed her going the other way.

"Take a picture, why don't you?" she challenged in return. She thought he was really gobbling the view . . . for a priest.

"A man never has a camera when he needs one," Paine replied, giving her one final overall and admiring examination before he quietly closed the door.

"What the hell's going on?" she demanded of the manager with her small fists balled on her bare hips. "Wally's a good customer, and we were just getting wound up!"

The brunette shushed her, slipped her a couple of hundreds, which calmed her quite a bit, and ushered her toward the front.

"What's up, sweetie?" Hapgood asked. He lay on his belly, naked, with his face turned toward the wall.

Paine thought, in passing, that he looked like a beached elephant seal.

"I don't think we know each other well enough for you to call me sweetie," Paine said.

15

"Judas priest!" Hapgood exclaimed, twisting his head around with enough violence to risk a cervical sprain.

"Not quite, Walter, but that's close," Paine replied. "I take it you weren't expecting me."

Hapgood raised himself up on his elbows on the massage table, then paused as he considered his next move. "What the hell are you doing here? We weren't scheduled to meet until tomorrow night!" The expression on Hapgood's face was a discordant mixture of shame, anger, fear, cunning, and surprize.

"I know," Paine replied, "but I just couldn't wait. From the look of that cutie I just saved you from, I would think remaining prone would be a real painful experience for you. My compliments on your taste in rubbers. She is definitely the pick of the litter."

"Rubbers?" Hapgood asked. The word seemed to strike him as one that had a special significance under the circumstances.

"Yeah. You know. Back-rubbers. That's what she was doing, wasn't it?" Paine inquired. He noticed the way Hapgood was casting longing glances at his clothing. It was all hanging from several hooks on the wall at the end of the room ten feet away.

"I don't think this is very funny, John. If you couldn't wait till tomorrow night, there were plenty of other places you could have chosen for our talk," Hapgood said. With some effort, he pushed himself up to a sitting position on the table.

"It's not meant to be funny, Walter. It's meant to be private, and that's what it is." Paine gestured toward the silent emptiness of the small space around them. "I'll hand you your clothes if that will spare you any further embarrassment."

"No!" Hapgood snapped. He raised a hand in sign that he could handle the task himself. "You needn't make me feel like a cripple as well as a buffoon!" The last thing Walter Hapgood wanted at that moment was for John Paine to touch his clothes. Because they contained what he now realized was his last chance to put Plan 'B' into effect.

With ample grumbling and complaint to cover the very real anxiety he was experiencing, Hapgood descended from the table under Paine's watchful eyes, and made his way to where his clothing was hung.

Hapgood's fright was an irrational one, based more on Paine's nature than on the likelihood that the rogue would recognize the "bug" he carried with him for what it was. The older man was far too practiced in such matters to choose a transmitter that looked like what it was. And given the high state of the art in covert electronics, it had been no challenge to equip himself with a device that even seasoned eyes would naturally dismiss.

Hapgood had decided to carry the specially adapted pen in his shirt pocket for the same reason that Paine had invented their scheduled rendezvous as a ruse. It was insurance against the possibility that the situation might take a sudden, unexpected turn for the worse. Paine might be the better soldier of the two, but he was not the only one who was wise enough to make provision for deception by a friend.

"How has Kevin been doing?" Paine asked as Hapgood donned his underwear and seated himself in the only available chair to pull on his socks. In fact, he knew how his partner was doing. Probably knew it much better than Hapgood did. But the continuing communication and friendship between them was a secret they no longer shared with anyone. Including his recruiter.

"You don't know, do you?" Hapgood asked rhetorically. "An attempt was made on his life only a few days ago, John. I'm sorry I didn't mention it before now." With his back to Paine, he slipped into the shirt, and as he was about to button it, depressed the switch on top of the pen that activated the signal to his wolves. He had commanded them to keep the alarm receiver with them at all times until Paine had been dealt with. And to never stray outside the beacon's range without his knowledge. In addition to the alarm, Strado and Thomas had a very expensive and effective tracking device that would enable them to find him within minutes if they rushed. Hapgood had stressed that he would not use it unless he was with Paine, and that if he did, and they did not arrive like the cavalry shortly thereafter, they should select their next favorite nation to call home.

"Is he all right?" Paine asked, trying to sound as convincingly surprized as he could.

"Yes. He's fine. He really acquitted himself in a way of which you would be proud. Very nearly killed the woman, from what I hear." Hapgood was able to relax somewhat once he had his pants on. There was something about being belted and zipped that made a man feel more equal to whatever it was he had to face. "You don't have any idea who she might have been, do you?"

"None at all," Paine lied. The mention of the attack by Vlota made him all the more glad that she had died as brutally as she had. "But I'm not surprized to hear that Kevin almost wasted her for her trouble. He's still more of a man in his condition than most." That part was, to his way of thinking, the truth.

When he was once again completely dressed, Hapgood felt confident enough to address Paine like the senior and elder man that he was. "I think you should seriously consider turning yourself in, John."

"Where have I heard that one before?" Paine replied. He leaned his shoulders back against the door and stared at Hapgood through the gloom with which the cubicle was filled.

"Yes. I know how you feel," Hapgood said.

"Do you, Walter? Really?" Paine's voice put a chill in the air. "Do you know what's it's like to be branded a traitor to the country you have served all your life? Do you know how it is to live every day of the week on the run? With no home, no friends, no rest? Have you been to purgatory, Walter? If you haven't, if you still have someone you can trust, someone who doesn't think you're no better than a mad dog that should be shot on sight, then don't tell me that you know how I feel. Because you don't. It's very cold out here, Walter. And I don't even know how I got here. All I know is that someone gave me a push when I wasn't looking. Then a bunch of other someones slammed the door before I could get back inside. Now everybody and his brother wants me dead. Why is that, Walter? How did I get so expendable so fast?"

Hapgood couldn't recall Paine ever saying that much at one time in the twenty-odd years he had known him. He found it all the more worrisome that the normally laconic operative had turned verbose.

"I'm sorry, John. You're right. I don't know how you feel. But I do know something that might change your mind about coming in," Hapgood said. His main interest was keeping Paine occupied until Strado and Thomas arrived, but he believed it was possible that he might be able to actually persuade the rogue to surrender himself by letting him know that his jeopardy was far greater than he knew. It was worth a try. Perhaps it would do no more than to crush Paine's indomitable will to survive, but that would be enough.

"I seriously doubt that, but you're free to give it your best shot," Paine said.

"On Brock's orders, Berghold has hired a contract agent to track you down," Hapgood said.

A silence ensued then between them. Paine knew what that meant.

"Is it Posey?" Paine asked. Cleetus Posey was the one man on earth who made his blood turn slushy in his veins. If Posey was after him, Paine knew it was time to get his affairs in order. That was how good he was. He never missed. Not ever. The Secret Service was afraid of Posey. They knew the President was a dead man if Posey came after him. Therefore, they had made it clear to the government of Sri Lanka, where Posey lived in a jungle redoubt, that if something so regrettable should occur, Sri Lanka would soon thereafter be the victim of a mysterious nuclear "accident" that would make it glow in the dark until the year 2234. Sri Lanka had, consequently, explained to

Posey that they would make *him* glow in the dark if they so much as heard a rumor to that effect. So there was a global agreement, to which Posey was a party, that he would content himself with targets whose friends could not retaliate on an Old Testament scale.

"No, John. Posey was not available," Hapgood said, having to conceal his regret. "Samson got the contract on you."

Paine breathed a sigh of relief. Samson was simply a remorseless, soulless, masterful psycopath. Besting him would be no Caribbean cruise, but he was up to it.

"You don't think I can handle Samson?"

"That's not the issue, John. If it were just you and him, I'd put all my money on you, of course. But it's not just the two of you, is it? You'll have to face him and all the other forces marshaled against you at the same time. Even *you* can only keep so many balls in the air before, inevitably, you let one of them drop. That's why my advice is that you find someone to surrender yourself to, before that happens." Hapgood left it at that, having said what he'd had to say. He estimated that fifteen minutes had passed since he'd sounded the silent alarm. He knew his war dogs must be closing in by now. It was time to put some space between himself and Paine, if at all possible, before they arrived. That would be the tricky part, and Walter Hapgood knew it. It meant risking giving the whole thing away, but to do otherwise would mean sharing the bulls-eye with Paine when the shooting started.

He found nothing sane about that prospect at all.

"Why don't you think it over, John, while I go wash up? Make yourself comfortable. I'll only be gone a few minutes," Hapgood said. He moved casually toward the door in front of which the agent stood.

"I've already thought it over long enough. My answer is still the same. So if our little talk is now concluded, I guess I will be on my way," Paine said. He was turning to let himself out when Hapgood blurted,

"No! Don't leave yet!" The words were barely out of his mouth when he realized he had just made the wrong move. In spades. But he hadn't expected Paine to suddenly decide to leave. That wasn't a part of the plan. The way the rogue had frozen in place where he stood made Hapgood fear that Paine had just realized that, too. A man who hadn't been behind a desk so long might have still salvaged things then by immediately reversing course, wishing Paine a fond farewell, and hoping for the best. But Hapgood panicked instead, let his mouth take over, and dug himself an even deeper hole. "Why don't you stick around and have some fun with one of the girls. Sherry, the one who was with me when you arrived, is as uninhibited as she is beautiful. Then there's blond Betsy. Or you might try them both. On me, of course!"

"What's wrong, Walter?" Paine asked quietly, turning back to face him. "Why is it so important for me to stick around? Why are you talking so fast?" He exhaled slowly as he reached a hand inside his coat for the acquisition he had made earlier in the day. A man could still purchase a shotgun and a spacious shoulder holster and carry both with him out of the store. Then he could buy a hacksaw and remove most of the barrel and all of the stock. It was only a twenty-gauge automatic, but it was enough. The six shells in its magazine could kick up quite a fuss in experienced hands.

"It's not what you think, John! So help me God!" Hapgood couldn't keep his voice from turning into a moan as he backed up to the wall. Strado and Thomas would be there at any moment, might be walking through the door even then. He couldn't take his eyes off of the murderous-looking shotgun-pistol in Paine's hand. To be shot with it at close range would mean a slow death, probably, and a messy one, from hemorrhage and shock.

"Why'd you do it, Walter?" There was genuine sadness and curiosity in Paine's voice. "What could be worth killing me for?" With his eyes on Hapgood, he focused his hearing on the interior of the small building. When he heard nothing at all, not even the limited background murmur of girlish chatter from the front, he realized his recruiter had somehow provided for the possibility that Paine would do what he had done. "I must apologize, Walter," Paine said, training the cavernous bore of the shotgun on the man's overstuffed midsection. "I've actually underestimated you. I didn't think I did that anymore, but apparently I do."

Hapgood was too petrified to trust his voice.

"Give it up, Paine!" A voice the rogue did not recognize hurled the command down the corridor in the best SWAT team fashion. "The building is surrounded!"

"How did you do it, Walter? Sincerely," Paine asked. When his recruiter made no reply, he added. "Don't worry. You can't make it any worse by telling me. Did I miss your surveillance? Or are you bugged?"

"I'm bugged" was Hapgood's forced reply.

Paine nodded his admiration. "Back off or Hapgood dies!" he bellowed.

"He's all yours, Paine!" Strado shouted back. "Feel free!"

The rogue smiled to himself darkly at that. It had been worth a try. He wondered if the building really was surrounded. Or if it was just the two he'd left alive at the church. There was no way for him to know. Hapgood was unlikely to admit to it if it was only the two.

"As soon as you shoot him, we shoot the girls, Paine! First one; then the other! You know we'll do it. Give it up, or civilians start to die!" Behind Strado, Thomas had the three young women lined up side by side on their faces on the floor. He had the muzzle of the Göncz assault pistol trained on the small of the brunette's back. His finger was snugged against the trigger.

Paine *did* know that they would do it. Something told him that the pair from the church were out there, regardless of whether they had a small army with them as they claimed. And he knew they were men much like himself—they didn't make empty threats—the principal difference between him and them being that they didn't mind wasting a few of the people they were sworn to protect. They were the new breed, the agents of the brave new world of the future, terrorists on the payroll of Uncle Sam.

First, they would kill the girls as a demonstration. If that didn't work, they would open fire on the cubicles where another half dozen or so taxpayers were cowering at that very moment. Or they might lob a few frags in, maybe some incendiaries. Whatever it took to insure that Paine didn't make it out alive.

And the rogue realized the likelihood of their success was greater than the likelihood of his. Rhonda's Retreat was not the World Trade Center. It was a small concrete box with one opening at each end. Under the circumstances, it reminded Paine of a roach motel for humans. You could either devastate the interior or fill it with tear gas and wait for the occupants to come staggering out into the hail of the awaiting guns.

Paine knew his only solid chance lay in taking advantage of all the other warm bodies around him to make good his escape. Once the screaming and bleeding and dying began, he could use the distraction to help him blast his way free of the trap. But to do so would mean descending to the level of terrorism himself. The genteel prostitutes and their johns whose lives now hung in the balance might not be pillars of morality, but they'd done nothing that merited execution. Not outside of Libya, at least.

Which meant, logically, that he had no valid choice but to surrender peacefully. It occurred to him that Hapgood's henchmen knew that. Knew they had the advantage on him, not only in years, but in ethics, too. If they'd considered him as much a shark as themselves, they wouldn't have wasted time on talk. They'd have simply opened fire.

"You chose your men well, Walter. They know my weak points. But they assume they have none. That may yet be their undoing. Still, it looks like you win this round. If I were you, though, I'd pray that they don't screw it up with me. Because if they do, you know what that will mean, don't you?" The look on Hapgood's face told him that his recruiter knew exactly what it would mean.

"All right!" Paine shouted.

"Toss the gun out where we can see it!" Strado replied.

Paine lobbed the Remington over the wall of the topless enclosure. A moment later he heard the thump when it landed in the hall.

"Now send Hapgood out!"

Paine beckoned the other man to him as he opened the door. Hapgood approached him as he would a coiled snake whose gleaming fangs were poised and extended. When they were face-to-face, the rogue reached out with both large hands toward Hapgood's throat and carefully adjusted the knot in his recruiter's tie.

"It's been a real education for me, Walter. I have a much better idea now who's behind my problems with the Company. I want you to know that I appreciate all that you've taught me. I feel I owe you a lot for that. I think you know me as a man who doesn't believe in letting such debts remain unpaid for very long." Paine looked into and through Hapgood's terrified eyes. "I'll be back, old friend. And when I return, there'll be no place for you to hide. Now go out there and tell your dogs to come and get their bone."

16

"Wake up, Paine! Time to suffer!" Thomas shouted into the rogue's face. Paine heard him, but only as a man at the bottom of a well hears another who is shouting down to him from its opening far above. He kept his eyes closed and his body still as his consciousness seeped slowly back into his mind. They'd injected him with something while he was spread-eagle against a wall at Rhonda's. Paine had been drugged enough times to recognize it as one of the opium derivatives. It had dropped him within seconds, and judging from the way he felt, he'd been out of it for hours.

"We're wasting our time," Strado remarked. He stood beside his partner, looking as bored as he felt. He'd gone along with the idea of debriefing Paine before they demoted him, but the later the hour became, the more his interest in the thing diminished.

"Are you kidding? There's no telling how much dirt this guy has to share with us!" Thomas looked at Strado sharply. He was convinced that they could squeeze Paine for secrets they could later use to their advantage in the Company.

Strado thought there was more to it than that, however. He believed that Thomas wanted to dote over their victim for a while as much as anything. It was, after all, a remarkable victory for two such junior operatives as themselves. So he was willing to go along with it for a while. He was honest enough to admit to himself that he didn't mind doing a little doting of his own. And there was no harm or risk involved, despite the fact that they were going against Hapgood's orders to simply terminate Paine and efficiently dispose of the remains. No one besides Paine and themselves would ever know about the interrogation, and Paine would be eternally unavailable for comment before long. The man also was too drugged to do anything but "hang around" while they questioned him. He was in no shape to take advantage of the brief stay in his execution. Even if he had been, however, Strado and Thomas were confident they could handle him as a team, regardless of how they would fare with him one on one.

"Maybe this will bring him around," Thomas said before he slammed a fist into the ugly purple discoloration that covered Paine's cracked ribs.

The rogue felt the pain, but it was a distant thing. So it was without too great effort that he checked his response to it. He must not let them know that he was rapidly regaining control of his faculties. The more alert he could become without their knowledge, the more likely he was to catch them unawares, and he badly needed the element of surprize to help equalize the advantage they had gained over him.

The closer to the surface he came, the greater the dimensions of that advantage appeared to be. For starters, there were the ribs that didn't feel cracked anymore...thanks to Brad Thomas. Even through the dense chemical haze, he could tell they were now broken. Which meant that every violent move he made would hurt plenty.

And every time a bolt of pain shot through him, he would lose a percentage of his strength. That was the way it worked with serious injuries. They tore at a man like hungry things with fangs until they wore him out and brought him down. Paine knew there was no resisting them for very long. So whatever he was going to do would have to be fast and efficient. There would be no Round Number Two.

His shoulders ached, and there was a sharper throbbing in his wrists, which told him they had somehow managed to hang him from his tethered hands. When he consulted his feet, they informed him they were dangling in the air.

"I bet if we remove his balls, he'll snap right out of it," Strado suggested quietly when Paine failed to respond.

"Probably," Thomas replied with a nod, "but as long as his pump is working, that will make a serious mess. To say nothing of what it would do to his ability to concentrate on our questions. Anyway, I don't think any carving will be necessary. He knows the way it works as well as anyone."

He was referring to the axiom in the game to the effect that *everybody* talks eventually, no matter how hard they might be. So coming clean at the start was the only sensible thing to do. Heroically forcing your interrogators to take you apart did no one any good. Least of all the one being questioned.

Paine *did* know that. He knew, too, however, that if the people grilling you had their hearts set on some juicy secrets, and you didn't know any, then the truth wouldn't help and you were in trouble deep. *Then* the only sensible thing was to act like John Le Carré and give them some quality fiction. This applied in spades when you knew you would live only as long as you had something interesting to say. When that was the case, as it was, then the story needed to be long as well as good.

Paine fought the narcotic urge to fall back into the sweet sleep from which he'd come. He refused to answer its soft lover's call to return to gentle velvet depths. He steeled himself and turned his attention to survival.

The three men made a strange scene in the midst of the vast, machine-filled processing floor. Strado and Thomas had removed only their coats for the interrogation. Paine was naked. He hung suspended from a sharp hook, part of the ceiling conveyer that carried sides of beef around the plant from one bloody butcher to another during the day. From a distance, the rogue looked like a carcass, and his captors might have been government inspectors checking to make sure he was fit to be consumed.

Strado had managed to gain access to the place that night by bribing the brother of one of his covey of girlfriends. The man was one of the plant's supervisors, and was more than a little awed when dealing with anyone who worked for the CIA. Strado had given him the standard song-and-dance about doing his patriotic duty while making a few tax-free bucks in the process. No embarrassing questions were asked, and that was just as well, since the answer Strado might have given him—if he had fallen prey to one of his rare attacks of honesty—was likely to have slaughtered the butcher's illusions about the Company on the spot.

"How much of that stuff did you give him, anyway?" Thomas asked Strado challengingly. "We could be here all night waiting for the guy to come around." Nervously he began to dance around on the balls of his feet, practicing his savate. He kicked Paine hard in one bare thigh, causing his big body to swing from side to side beneath the hook.

"I tripled the recommended dose for putting the average man in lullabye land for a while," Strado replied evenly. "I figured it would either kill him or make him very manageable till we were ready to pull his plug. Big John here is famous for his ability to bounce back from almost anything. But I don't think he's going to be bouncing back from this."

"Tell me, Vincent, are we bad, or are we bad?" Thomas stopped kicking Paine long enough to slap hands with his partner.

"We are bad," Strado acknowledged. "I really thought it would be tougher to put Paine away than this." He glanced at the massive, inert form with an expression that was nearly one of disappointment.

"Another myth bites the dust, my man," Thomas said sympathetically. "And the heavyweight crown is passed to those who really deserve it. I told you he was living on faded glory. Weren't you, Johnny Boy?" Thomas moved to Paine's side as he plucked a button knife from his back pocket. "Rise and shine, old man!" With his left hand, he lifted the rogue's lolling head, brought the knife close to it, and released the spring-loaded blade. It whipped free and locked into position with a sharp metallic snap. The six-inch chromed length gleamed with the cold reflected light from the banks of neon suspended from the ceiling above.

Paine groaned to let Thomas know he was coming around. There was no telling what the young hotshot might do to rouse him if he suddenly ran out of patience. The rogue didn't need to open his eyes to know the sound of a switchblade opening. There was no other sound quite like it.

"Let's get this over with," Strado said. He moved to Brad Thomas's side in front of Paine. "I'm not looking forward to what we have to do, so I'd like to just do it, and quit screwing around." Strado's eyes were on Paine's face as he spoke. He was frankly disgusted by what they had planned. It was his partner's idea. But a good one, in his opinion. Paine needed to disappear without a trace... like Jimmy Hoffa. That was the only way to insure that there would never be any embarrassing repercussions from any quarter regarding his termination. There was no pleasant way for that to be accomplished. But there was one that was *guaranteed*.

"Relax, Vince. If your stomach can't handle it, mine can." Thomas, too, was watching Paine's face as he spoke. He pressed the point of the blade into the soft tissue behind Paine's chin and worked it around until it broke the skin.

Even before his eyes flickered open, the rogue knew to what sort of place they had taken him... and why. The smell of death and dismemberment was a rank and cloying thing that drenched the air around them. Hapgood's ambitious thugs weren't about to settle for his torment and his death. They were too ruthlessly efficient for that. Before they were through with him, his flesh would be indistinguishable from the rest of the pulverized tissue that got carted to the dump each day.

"Welcome back, Big John!" Thomas said when Paine was able to focus on him with a difficulty that was apparent. Thomas pushed the tip of the knife in a bit deeper when it looked like Paine was going to fade. "That was first-class dope, wasn't it? Nothing but the best for our victims, pal. Now it's Q-and-A time, Paine. We 'Q,' and you 'A.' Got that?"

Paine responded with a boozy nodding of his

head that was part act and part opiate.

"Speak up, Johnny!" Strado jabbed a fist into Paine's scrotum hard enough to start his body swinging again.

"Go for it, Vinnie! Let's see some of those patented moves!" Thomas bobbed out of the way when he realized Strado was about to work out some of his frustrations on the helpless Paine. The rogue gasped convincingly as the agony from his pounded testicles roared through him. He was still reeling from the first blow when it was followed by another to his gut. Strado used Paine as a punching bag, slashing and hooking and hammering, moving around him in a boxer's crouch. Every blow was expertly aimed for maximum effect.

"All right! All right! What do you want to know?" Paine's words were an anguished roar. He knew he could not take such enthusiastic punishment for too long without getting more badly hurt than he already was. They could work on his face all night if they wanted to, but he couldn't afford to have his plumbing rearranged. That would put him out of action for good.

Strado stopped hitting him then and positioned himself directly in front of the rogue for the interrogation.

"Who are you really working for, Paine? Lay it out for us nice and simple, and you can get it over with. We'll make it quick for you then. I give you my word on that," Strado told him. His hard black eyes were as brutal in their own way as his fists.

"He speaks the truth, old man," Thomas added. "I don't want to bum you out, but this butcher shop is where your personal story is about to reach its conclusion. You've probably figured that out for yourself by now, but if not, there it is. You're going to die here, and then I'm going to dice you up so I don't have to worry about your coming back to haunt me someday. That's pretty grim, I know, but believe me when I tell you it will be even grimmer if we think you're trying to hold out on us," Thomas said. He addressed Paine patronizingly, as if the man who so outranked him in experience and accomplishment were no more than a large helping of living garbage that was sorely in need of disposal.

Paine decided then that he wanted to save Brad Thomas for last. He wanted to devote a little extra time and attention to him if he could. For all the disrespect. He found such sneering more annoying than all of Strado's vicious blows.

"I won't hold out on you," Paine said, slurring his words as if the dope's hold on him were still greater than it was. He wasn't entirely free of it, though, and he was glad that he was not. Along with the fuzzing of his thoughts, the drug that still coursed through him was significantly limiting his body's pain. As long as the sluggishness didn't cripple him, that anesthesia would work to his advantage. "I've been working for the Mossad for five years."

"The Mossad, huh?" Strado responded. He looked at his partner as if to say, Who would ever have guessed? "Very interesting. Who recruited you?"

"Chaim Weitzman," Paine responded. "He's a double for the KGB, I think. I don't know for sure." He was making it up as he went. All that mattered was making it interesting and complicated. If it was interesting, they would want to hear more. If it was complex, it would take some time to tell it. If it took long enough, one of them was likely to leave the room eventually. That was what he was waiting for. He had to get one of them alone, and he hoped the one he got would be Strado.

For nearly an hour he plied them with lies as only a practiced, professional liar could. From time to time he would lapse into silence, his breathing labored as if the combination of exhaustion, injury, and overdose were overwhelming him. One look at him was proof in itself that he was well past his prime, beaten, and knew it.

Thomas and Strado were steadily seduced as Paine intended. As in all such seductions, they were unwitting accomplices because he was giving them what they wanted: "secrets" and submission. The more he divulged, and the lower he seemed to sink, the more pleased with themselves and contented his persecutors became. It was a natural and predictable process to the rogue. He had used it before on interrogators both older and wiser than Hapgood's dynamic duo.

The only real booby traps that were built into such situations were, first, running out of palatable lies, and second, getting too Shakespearean with the "whipped dog" routine. Paine knew he could probably have begged and sobbed and generally given the whole show away with a pair of virgins like Strado and Thomas without them seeing through it. But it was not a time for underestimating them as they were underestimating him. So he kept the cornucopia of fabrications rolling while he maintained the show of a former tough guy who was doing his best to hold on to the remnants of his pride to the bitter end.

When Thomas finally said, "I need to take a leak. Where the hell is the john in this place, Vince?" Paine's occasional belief that some Providence still functioned in the universe in favor of the just was significantly renewed.

"It's out in the hall down at that end," Strado replied with a pointing gesture toward his left.

As Thomas turned and walked away, Paine

said, "You got a cigarette for me, Vince?" He hoped the humble request would serve to put Strado further off guard. The man gave him an icy look at first, but then he shrugged and fished a smoke and his lighter out of his shirt pocket.

"Sure. Why not?" Strado said. As he lit the cigarette, Paine turned his head slightly to watch Thomas crossing to the distant door. His eyes never left Strado, however, as he relied on his peripheral vision to follow the other man out of the room. Strado had just placed the filter between Paine's lips when the sound of the closing door resonated throughout the enclosure.

"Thanks," Paine muttered gratefully around the cigarette as Strado took one backward step away. Then Paine slammed the top of his right foot up into Strado's balls with every ounce of strength that his great body possessed. The maneuver was impaired by the way he was suspended from his wrists. That made the necessary leverage a challenge. It worked well enough, however, to lift Vince Strado off the floor before dumping him on his back in a fetal posture with a severe case of the dry heaves.

But even as Strado retched, he was struggling to reach his gun as Paine hung there waiting to get shot.

Paine looked up at the hook from which he dangled, praying that he was still as athletic as he needed to be.

17

"Hurts something fierce, doesn't it, Vince?" Paine growled. He kicked both feet up toward the conveyor, and the instant before he reached it, a great dull sledgehammer of pain reached his brain from the broken ribs. He snarled, trying to ignore the agony . . . and failing. He let his legs drop, hanging there still for a moment as he waited for the long teeth biting him to set him free. A few feet away on the floor, Strado had his automatic in his hand. He lay there gagging and trying to push himself up to a firing position. Both men knew a contest to the death had just begun. The first one to overcome the injury that crippled him would immediately bring the other's suffering to a sudden, savage stop.

Paine took a long, deep breath and slowly blew it out.

Strado moaned as he rolled himself by force of will onto his hands and knees. He sat up, clutching at his groin, his torso canted at an odd angle to his legs. "Son of a bitch!" he groaned.

Paine launched both bare feet up toward the track from which he hung. His heels found and locked around it. The jagged bones in his side ground together and threatened to drop him again. It felt like a bayonet being driven into him repeatedly. His big body was suddenly bathed in sweat as he clung there high above the floor like a monstrous spider. He clenched his teeth, his arms and legs shaking as he forced his ankles over the conveyor to lock above it and momentarily take his weight.

Strado lifted the automatic. The muzzle wandered as the waves of raging nausea continued thundering through him. His eyes were full of tears. He had to pause for seconds to scrub them with a wrist to clear them.

Paine slipped the nylon rope that bound his wrists up off of the hook. Then he seized the hook with both hands, unlocked his ankles, and snarled as he let his body drop and the ribs once again exploded.

When he let go of the hook and his feet hit the floor, Vince Strado had the nine-millimeter leveled on his chest. Strado managed a dark smile through the pain as he squeezed the trigger. When nothing happened, both men remained frozen for a moment.

Strado's smile faded as Paine grabbed a machete-sized butcher knife that lay gleaming wickedly on top of a stainless steel table beside him.

There was ten feet between them.

Strado was fumbling to release the safety when Paine barked, "You *lose*, pal!" and hurled the heavy blade with a single sweeping pitch of his long right arm.

The point took Strado in the center of his chest, slicing through everything in the way as it was designed to do, penetrating until it slammed into his spine and half its length was sheathed in his flesh.

Vincent Strado completely forgot about his

mashed nuggets as he stared down at the wooden handle that projected from his bloodstained shirt. Then he forgot about the gun, as well, and let it drop. Both hands found the handle, as with a will of their own, and closed around it as if he might pull it free in the short time he had left.

Paine crossed to where the dying man knelt, looking like the world's most determined suicide, and picked up the gun. "I'd like to hang around and watch you croak, stud, but it's time to give some of the same to your friend. So you're on your own, Vince." Their eyes joined as he allowed himself a brief gloat, and the younger man showed him he still had enough life left in him to hate.

"He'll kill you," Strado gasped.

"In a pig's ass," Paine replied. "He's dead meat ...just like you."

Thomas was through the door before he saw Strado lying on his back with the butcher knife rising like a harpoon from his chest. That image registered at the same instant as the touch of the muzzle of his partner's automatic nine against the side of his head.

"Vince is resting while he rots," Paine said quietly. "He just got himself wasted by an *old man*, Thomas, the one who still happens to be the heavyweight champ. Lose the gun, son." When Thomas hesitated, Paine added, "This piece is cocked. Do you really think you're that fast?"

Thomas didn't. He carefully removed the automatic from his belt holster in the prescribed manner and tossed it a safe distance to his right.

Then Brad Thomas smiled. "What do we do now, *champ*?"

"Take a couple of steps to your right and face me," Paine said.

Thomas did so as he continued to smile. The

man he looked at was still naked, but that didn't seem to bother him much. Not nearly as much, certainly, as the broken and abused ribs.

"I don't want to bum you out, but this is where your personal story reaches its conclusion," Paine said, quoting Thomas's own words back to him.

"Oh, I see. You're going to rub it in for a few minutes, right? I can appreciate that," Thomas said with a nod.

"I think you should be in a suitably respectful frame of mind when you go to join Vince in worm country," Paine said.

"If it makes you feel better, I now know you're as good as your reputation. I mean that. I should have killed you back at the massage parlor." Thomas shrugged, and his smile took on a wry cast.

"Yeah. You should have. Hapgood fed you to me. Do you know that, too?" Paine kept the gun aimed at the center of the agent's body.

"Yeah. That sounds pretty close. Give him my regards when you see him, okay?" Thomas looked into Paine's eyes for understanding, killer to killer, and found it.

"Sure thing," Paine said. "Do you want to get it over with now? I know that's grim, but your only other option is even grimmer." The look he gave Thomas held a fatal, roguish challenge.

"You're really a nasty man, Paine. What's the option?"

"A shot at the title. Think you're up to it?" It was what Paine wanted; to punish Thomas for his insolence. But he would leave it up to him. He wasn't too sore to simply settle for killing him.

"Oh, yeah," Thomas said with a chuckle, "I'm up to it. You're the one with the handicap." A glint had come to his eyes at the prospect of a duel between the two of them. Was it possible that

Paine would take him on, man to man, with the broken ribs? If he would, Thomas was confident that he could kill him.

"Don't worry about my handicap, Thomas. Which way will it be? Easy or hard?"

"I never could resist a challenge. Let's do it," Thomas replied.

"Remember, you asked for it," Paine said. Then he shot Thomas through the right shoulder. "Now we're even."

Paine hurled Strado's weapon away to clatter to the floor among the machines and advanced on his wounded opponent.

Thomas pushed himself back up to his feet from the knee on which he dropped when he was shot. He cursed the man coming toward him, baring his teeth against the agony from the shattered shoulder. Blood coursed from the wound down his arm and onto the floor.

Then Brad Thomas started to dance. He bounced gracefully from foot to foot, trying to find his balance in spite of the wound. He might have lost the use of his arm, but he was a kick-boxer, and there was nothing wrong with either of his legs.

Paine lumbered toward him flatfooted, the ribs causing him observable trouble with every step.

Thomas reminded himself that the rogue hadn't freed himself and killed Strado by being as clumsy as he looked. Thomas's shoulder was swiftly numbing as his mind's automatic damage-control mechanism kicked in. He feinted toward his opponent to throw Paine off balance, then fired a kick at his injured ribs. To Thomas's surprise, Paine made no attempt to avoid the blow. He blocked it with a thick forearm instead and made a grab for the flicking foot.

Paine knew he couldn't match Thomas for speed

and grace. But he knew, too, that he outweighed him by sixty pounds and was twice as strong. Paine also knew how to take a licking and keep on ticking. It was a favorite, if unorthodox, weapon against younger and more agile opponents like Thomas.

The way it worked was, he got beat-up, and they got killed. Paine found that acceptable in spite of the expense.

Thomas recognized the strategy fast. Paine stalked him like a relentless wounded bear. It was a shuffling, brutal, hypnotic fighting style reminiscent of Joe Frazier in his prime. Like Frazier, Paine let Thomas take his best shots, occasionally reeling, sometimes forced to defend himself from an especially fast and vicious combination, but never varying his style, always wading forward.

After a few minutes, the fatigue and frustration started to set in with Thomas. Paine was waiting him out, and Thomas knew it. He was waiting for a single opening to finish it. The man could absorb punishment in a way Thomas had thought impossible. He could drive Paine to his knees, then kick him in the head, and the invincible bastard would shake it off and struggle back to his feet.

It was going on too long, Thomas realized. He was slowing down; his reactions were becoming as sluggish as Paine's. The blood loss and trauma from the point-blank bullet were about to turn him into a plodding wreck like his opponent. When that happened, the contest would become one of brawn and endurance, and that would seal his fate since Paine outclassed him in both categories.

Thomas shifted to the defensive, circling the rogue and feinting a kick now and then as he concentrated on finding a weapon with which he could regain the advantage. He searched the floor whenever he could for the gun he'd been forced to discard, but like "Smokin' Joe" himself, John Paine never let him relax. The sweating, weary hulk was always in his face, swinging at him with his strong-side fist and launching his own array of kicks, any one of which would cripple if Thomas took it fully. The man might not be a ballerina, but there was a certain programmed poise to his movements that never left him. As a dance partner, he was no match for Fred Astaire, but if necessary, Paine could dance right through a wall. Without missing a step on his way through.

When Thomas gave up on looking for the gun and settled for snatching up a meat cleaver from its rack as he passed, Paine smiled behind his straining face. Because he knew he had him then. He knew his young opponent was running out of gas, getting scared and desperate.

Paine stopped then. The two men stood facing each other, heaving for breath, suffering mightily from their respective wounds, separated by little more than the length of a long arm.

"Come on, Thomas! Do it!" Paine wheezed. "For once in your slimy life, act like a man! Show me what you've got! You want the crown...*punk*! So come and take it from me! I dare ya!" He had to force the words out between ragged breaths. The exhaustion was no act, but the challenge was pure theater. He wanted Brad Thomas to lose that excellent cool of his...just once...under extreme pressure...and throw himself into Paine's open arms and his own demise.

And Brad Thomas did just that.

"You mother!" Thomas snarled. To his credit, he didn't charge like a bull. He double-feinted on the way in, raising the cleaver above his head as if to strike overhand, then lunging to Paine's weak side before suddenly shifting to the strong side

179

and dropping the cleaver for a wicked horizontal slash intended to turn Paine's broad belly into a great vomiting mouth.

Paine resisted the instinctive urge to take the bait and move according to Thomas's plan. He stood his ground instead, remaining still as stone until the younger man committed himself and swung the cleaver low for the gutting stroke. Then Paine countered with a savage chopping forearm aimed at the streaking wrist. A miscalculation would mean learning to live with one less hand, but he did not miscalculate. The point of impact was where he meant it to be; the cleaver flew from Thomas's hand, and Paine seized him by the arm and had him.

Thomas fought him desperately like a hooked trout, as Paine twisted the arm up behind his back and threw a hydraulic hammerlock around his neck, pulling the man's back against his chest.

"Time to suffer! Wasn't that how you put it?" Paine snarled into Thomas's ear. He picked him up despite the roaring pain from his ribs and toted him to one of the industrial appliances in the immediate vicinity that Paine found deeply appealing at the time.

When Thomas realized what was coming, he began to scream. And beg. And plead.

Paine used his knee to flick the switch that made the apparatus come to life. It made a large, electric, inhuman sound as the gears whirled and the blades spun inside the spacious hopper that yawned at the end of a table like a beast that couldn't wait for the next tender morsel to be dropped in.

"I told you there was an easy way and a hard way, kid," Paine growled into Thomas's ear as he slowly folded him toward the hopper. Thomas shrieked as Paine pushed his face down toward the shining blur designed to convert whatever it was fed into a fine pink pulp. "This is the hard way." Paine pulled his arm out of the way and put his hand on the back of Thomas's head. "I think a man who wants to be a hot dog ought to get his wish, Thomas. Presto chango! You're a hot dog, amigo!"

Paine gave Thomas's head a good, hard shove down to the fate he deserved.

Being as neat as he was by nature, John Paine was inclined to haul what was left of Hapgood's bloodhounds to the reefer where all the other carcasses were stored before he left. Considering the sort of men they were, he thought it would be an appropriate resting place for both. Hanging side by side on adjoining hooks. But there was too little left of him for even the most poetic of gestures, so he settled for leaving them where they lay.

He found it hard enough to dress and drag himself from the charnel house that had nearly been the end for him instead.

By the time he found a phone, even identifying himself was suddenly a serious challenge.

"It's Father John. You doing anything?" he asked.

"Waiting to find out that you're alive," Chita Torres answered. "You don't sound so good."

"You should see the way I look," Paine groaned.

"I'd like to," Chita said softly.

"I'll see what I can do," Paine replied, before he hung up the phone and promptly collapsed.

EPILOGUE

"You're free to go," the detective said. He was unable to conceal the combination of relief and revulsion he was feeling at the time. He'd never been forced to have such a man in custody as his responsibility, and he vowed to retire before allowing it to happen again. "All those papers of yours and the people you said would vouch for you have checked out." The Homicide veteran was tempted to say much more; was tempted to ask the little nightmare standing before him if the Feds did business regularly with denizens of the Underworld like himself. But the wheels that had slowly turned to set the assassin free were very large wheels indeed. The order to release the man had come to One Police Plaza from Washington, D.C. Rumor had it that the command had been couched in less than diplomatic terms: leave him strictly alone, regardless of what he has done or what he may do ... unless you have lost interest in keeping your job.

The fact that the scary elf from Hell had killed two drugged-up thugs who mistook him for a human being and tried to push him around on his first night in jail was completely irrelevant. As was the undisputed evidence that he had wasted four gang members on the Lower East Side on the night of his arrest.

It was a situation unlike any the detective had ever encountered before, and it smelled as bad as the East River at its worst. No one should be above the law, least of all the faceless psycho he was setting free, but that made the license to kill he carried with him no less valid that it had turned out to be. What was the world coming to, the detective wondered, when such evil arrangements were made . . . for *any* reason? And what could possibly justify a marriage between the government and a walking argument in favor of capital punishment like the man who stood looking up at him with nothing recognizably human behind his blood-colored eyes?

That was one of the few questions the detective could recall asking himself in recent memory, the answer to which was both obvious and irrefutable. *Nothing*. Nothing could justify climbing into the sack with such a mutation.

"It has been less than a pleasure, Lieutenant," Samson said softly, "but I suppose you know that, don't you? Please tell the chef for me that a slow death from his own cooking would be no less than he deserves."

What passed for Samson's mouth warped into what might have been intended as a smile. "Now, if you will excuse me, I must return to what I was doing before your *colleagues* chose to interrupt me. I must find a man and discuss his sins with him. Sins of the mortal kind." Samson's lashless lids flickered spastically over his bottomless burgundy eyes. "The sort that men like you and I . . . and him . . . specialize in."

God forbid I should share a category with you, the detective thought, and heaven help whoever it is you seek.

#1

HIS THIRD CONSECUTIVE NUMBER ONE BESTSELLER!

James Clavell's

WHIRLWIND

70312-2/$6.99 US/$7.99 CAN

From the author of *Shōgun* and *Noble House*—
the newest epic in the magnificent Asian Saga
is now in paperback!

"WHIRLWIND IS A CLASSIC—FOR OUR TIME!"
Chicago Sun-Times

WHIRLWIND

is the gripping epic of a world-shattering upheaval that
alters the destiny of nations. Men and women barter for
their very lives. Lovers struggle against heartbreaking odds.
And an ancient land battles to survive as a new reign of
terror closes in . . .

FROM PERSONAL JOURNALS TO BLACKLY HUMOROUS ACCOUNTS

VIETNAM

DISPATCHES, Michael Herr
01976-0/$4.50 US/$5.95 Can
"I believe it may be the best personal journal about war, any war, that any writer has ever accomplished."
—Robert Stone, *Chicago Tribune*

M, John Sack
69866-8/$3.95 US/$4.95 Can
"A gripping and honest account, compassionate and rich, colorful and blackly comic."
—*The New York Times*

ONE BUGLE, NO DRUMS, Charles Durden
69260-0/$4.95 US/$5.95 Can
"The funniest, ghastliest military scenes put to paper since Joseph Heller wrote *Catch-22*"
—*Newsweek*

AMERICAN BOYS, Steven Phillip Smith
67934-5/$4.50 US/$5.95 Can
"The best novel I've come across on the war in Vietnam"
—Norman Mailer